# The Case of the Hexed Heart

The Feline Files - Book 2

K.E. O'Connor

K.E. O'Connor Books

ISBN: 978-1-918248-00-5

THE CASE OF THE HEXED HEART

**For Minnie**

To a remarkable black and white cat who saw the
world through one brilliant eye but with twice
the spirit of any ordinary feline. Master escape
artist, snackie connoisseur, and the queen of
sass, you made every day an adventure with your
mischievous heart and endless capacity for joy.

This story is for you, little furry queen.

# Chapter 1

My ears lowered as the rain lashed against the cracked library windowpanes. It had been raining in Badger's Haze for approximately three million days, give or take. At least, that's what it felt like.

I'd barely left the library because every time I went out, I'd return soaked and shivering with icy cold toe beans, and I had no wonderful witch to pat me dry with a soft towel straight from the dryer.

I had to stay healthy. If I caught any illness while stuck in Badger's Haze, there was no telling what would happen to me. The locals were still wary of me, despite saving their miserable existence from an eternity of servitude by a deranged spider-like entity, and that meant I'd be alone, with no one bringing me homemade chicken soup and rubbing my back.

A loud thud, followed by a clatter of books tumbling from the shelves, had me turning with my fur bristling. "Stop reenacting that historical duel. You know it never ends well."

For the last few days, the scholarly ghosts I shared the library with had attempted to entertain me by putting on shows of epic battles from history, including the Battle of Holy Frost Thaw, the Great Sasquatch Raids of the First Witch Era, and the Battle of Glenda the Elder.

It could have been fun, but they were cautious about the weapons they used, preferring floating quills instead of spells, swords, or barbed ice spears.

Mind you, a carefully aimed quill hitting one's head had a jarring effect even if it was thrown by a weak-muscled ghost who preferred books to exercise.

I stared at the books lying forlornly on the floor. If Vorana Stowell were here, she'd be furious at such mistreatment of precious paper. But she was in my beloved and much-missed hometown of Crimson Cove, a place I was officially banished from going near.

A breath huffed out of me. That banishment needed to be overturned as soon as possible.

Dodging another falling book, I left the ghosts to their own devices and strode to the often malfunctioning but most important snow globe. I tapped it firmly with a white paw.

Sage, my curmudgeonly best friend and only contact in Crimson Cove, shimmered into view a few seconds later. She was chewing something. That cat never stopped eating. Although when she paused from her gluttony, it was to fall asleep. Sage slept long and hard. She loved a nap.

"Greetings!" I said. "I'm assuming that no news is good news. I've barely heard from you in over a week."

"Not my fault. It's the annual Crimson Cove Book Fair," Sage said. "Vorana has barely slept. She's been so excited. We had daily talks, and the place was so busy that the bookshelves were almost empty."

I sighed, not even attempting to hide my displeasure at missing out on such a treat. "I take it there were food stalls, too?"

"Of course. We're working our way through the yummy leftovers," Sage said. "Sorcha even got extra help at the café because it was so full-on. She set up a stall outside too. Her vampy boyfriend looked after it in the evening, so no one missed out on treats."

"Except me. Did my wonderful witch buy any books?" I asked.

"She poked her head in the store a couple of times, but said she didn't like crowds," Sage replied. "Actually, Zandra's not been around much recently."

I settled onto a heap of old newspapers. "That's because she's been here. Although not here, here. I didn't see her, but there was a thunderous noise at the border two nights ago, so I know she was trying to break through."

Sage winced. "I wondered if she'd make it in this time."

"You knew Zandra had a plan to break me out?" I asked.

"Vorana tried to talk her out of it, but Zandra was convinced she'd found a spell that would get you free. She must have magicked herself over there and tried breaking through the barrier."

"My witch is truly magnificent, but since I'm still stuck, she failed this time," I said.

"If Angel Force caught her, she'll be in a cell," Sage said. "Last time Zandra got caught trying to break through, it took five angels to drag her back to Crimson Cove and lock her up."

"They'd better not have harmed my witch," I growled. "She's only doing this to help me."

"Finn makes sure everything is handled fairly," Sage said. "He'll never let Zandra come to harm."

"But she'll never give up, so the punishment will only get worse." I didn't want to think of Zandra stuck in a cell because of me.

"We've tried talking sense into her, but we don't want to see you decaying in Badger's Haze forever."

"I won't! And I'll find a way home," I said. "Can't the angels see I'm helping? We solved an unsolvable case for them. You are reminding them of that daily, aren't you? You're putting up banners? Getting the *Free Juno* petition signed? What about social media? We could start an online video campaign."

"I visit the Angel Force office daily and get the door shut in my face," Sage said. "I never knew angels could be so rude."

"That's Cythera's fault." My paws flexed. I'd have words with those angels when I got out of here. They were slow-moving creatures and adored their bureaucracy, but they must see I was a decent, mostly law-abiding, magical cat. I was a help, not a hindrance.

"I thought marrying Maverick would have softened her," Sage said. "And it did for a short time, but the higher angels are still floating in, poking about and asking questions, so she's back to her usual, craggy self."

"We need to get more inventive," I said. "You really have to start a petition. Have the entire town of Crimson Cove sign it to say I must be set free, or they'll strike."

Sage snort-laughed. "They won't do that. Sure, we'll get some names, but not enough to worry Angel Force."

"Then set up a noisy protest outside their office," I said. "Chain yourself to the door and refuse to leave until they free me."

"And miss naptime and snackies? I like you, but not that much," Sage said.

I turned my back for a second, overcome with frustration. I had to get Angel Force to see sense. There had been crossed wires when I'd saved Crimson Cove from a dark power that slid into the town because of me, but I wasn't totally to blame. I hadn't created the darkness, and I'd done everything to destroy it.

Admittedly, I was almost too late in figuring things out, but I was on the side of good. Those stuffy, feather-headed angels couldn't see that. And they wouldn't see it until I stood in front of them and laid everything out in simple terms even they could understand.

"Am I going to have to talk to your rear end for the rest of this conversation? You have a cute butt, but it's hard to figure out your mood just looking at the fluff," Sage said.

Another pile of books crashed off a shelf, making me jump. I turned around.

"What have you got going on there?" Sage asked.

"The library ghosts are entertaining me," I muttered. "It's going poorly. But since there's nothing else to do around here, I'm stuck with my scholarly ghostly companions."

"You're still getting trouble from the locals?"

"I haven't seen anyone to get trouble from," I said. "A cloud of rainy despair has settled over Badger's Haze. It's wiped away the fog, but it's brought torrential rain, and it's not leaving anytime soon. Everyone is hiding inside."

Sage poked out her tongue. "I hate rain almost as much as I hate baths."

"You enjoy a good bubble bath," I said.

"So do you. You just don't like to admit it."

I flicked an ear. "I don't always object to Zandra's scented bubbles. And I'd agree to having a daily bath if it meant I could get out of here."

"I wouldn't lead with that negotiating offer when facing off with the angels," Sage said.

I wrinkled my booping snooter. "There's only one thing for it."

"What have you got in mind?"

"We solve another cold case."

# Chapter 2

Sage sighed long and hard, like she was going for an Olympic medal in familiar huffing, then nodded. "I know there's no point in telling you not to. You had one picked out, didn't you? What's the victim's name?"

"Doctor Iona Wren." I tapped the case file I'd set on the desk.

"And what's so special about this one?"

"There's something about the case that sent a chill down my spine," I said. "She was a renowned magical healer. Powerful and well respected. Someone who should have been protected rather than murdered."

"What did Angel Force think the cause of death was?" Sage asked.

I nudged the file closer and flipped through the pages. "Natural causes with possible magical influence."

Sage snort-smirked. "That's a cop-out sentence if ever I've heard one."

"I was suspicious as soon as I read that vague phrase," I said. "And the case was closed almost as soon as it was opened."

"Do you think an angel was involved?" Sage asked. "They were protecting one of their own, so they did the basics and then shut things down."

"No, but as usual, I feel Angel Force was out of its depth," I said. "They found a puzzling crime, couldn't fit the pieces together, and despite interviewing witnesses and suspects, they closed it with no progress made. I suspect ninety percent of the files Angel Force looks into follow the same path."

"That's unnecessarily mean," Sage said. "They do their best."

"I'm allowed to be mean. They banished me to a cursed village where it's permanently foggy, raining, and generally gross. The people are mean, the food is lousy, and I have no friends here."

"That's not such a bad thing. The friend you made recently turned into an unhinged killer," Sage said.

"I make dreadful choices when it comes to my friends." I gave an overly theatrical sigh.

"Same here," Sage said. "My friendships always lead me into trouble."

"Not anymore, they don't," I replied. "Not with me stuck here."

"You're not my only friend," Sage said. "But you're one of the few I fully trust."

Although Sage could be as grumpy as the day was long and twice as surly, I valued her friendship like nothing else. She was the only one I'd been able to contact since being banished to Badger's Haze, but our snow globe connection was wonky at the best of times. I never knew when we'd get to spend more than a few minutes talking.

"I can see your weirdo ghosts dueling with what look like feather quills," Sage said.

"They do that. I've tried ignoring them, but it only makes them more inventive. I'm letting them get on with it."

One of my regular library ghosts surged forward and swirled around my head. It was Professor Craggleton, who had a particular love for spouting obscure twelfth-century poetry at deafening volumes, mispronouncing half the words.

"Don't go stirring trouble," he whispered in my ear.

"I could say the same for you," I said. "Aren't you bored with your battle reenactments yet?"

He twirled around me, leaving white trails of spectral goo that dripped onto the floor. "Dr. Wren was trouble."

That got my attention. "What do you know about her?"

"I know that if you poke a mystery like that, it will bite back." He whirled around me one more time before zooming off, cackling to himself.

"Now I'm interested," Sage said.

"Same here," I replied. "This cold case is from 2001, so the tests done could have missed something. It's worth looking into, especially given the curious nature of how Angel Force closed it. Iona's killer is out there. Perhaps they're even still living in Badger's Haze. We could be neighbors."

"I can do some research from this end," Sage said. "Is there anything in particular you want me to look into?"

"There was a brooch found at the crime scene." I flipped over a few more pages. "An heirloom brooch known as the hexed heart was found on the body. There was an old brooch with a red stone in the box file, but there's not a hint of magic in it. At least, not that I sense. That could be connected to this case. It's pretty with gold swirls on it, but not powerful. Not anymore."

"The hexed heart?" Sage scratched at her ear with a front paw. "That rings a bell. And anything hexed needs to be approached with caution."

"The locals gave it that nickname, and it stuck."

"Still... why not pick something less deadly?"

"I have nothing better to do. And if we solve this mystery, Angel Force will finally see sense and realize they can't do without me. And it's good news for you. You won't have to chain yourself to their office door and beg for my safe return."

"Nothing will convince me to chain myself to anything." Sage's head turned. "I hear a can being opened. It's time for my second dinner and then a nap. What have you got tonight?"

"I've been ransacking abandoned houses," I said. "I found a treat. There was a giant pile of tinned ham. The tins have easy-open hooks, so I can open them without too much trouble."

"That sounds disturbingly gross," Sage said. "I'll stick to my steak. Vorana's cutting it up for me so I don't have to slurp it too much."

I tried not to drool and ignored my grumbling stomach at the thought of a delicious steak, served medium-rare and dripping in butter.

"You'll get heartburn if you eat too quickly," I said.

"When have you known me to eat too quickly?" Sage asked. "I've got teeth for grinding these days. Perhaps I should become a vegetarian."

I grimaced. "Let's not be unreasonable. Enjoy your steak."

"Enjoy your tinned ham. Send me the case file. I'll read it while I eat." Sage disconnected.

After pressing the send button and shaking the globe to ensure it did what it was supposed to, I settled down, attempting to block out the thunderous rain that sounded like it wanted to smash through the window and drench me, and started reading what I hoped would be the case that paved the way home.

**Case file:** #2001-1020
**Date filed:** October 20, 2001

**Victim information**

**Name:** Wren, Dr. Iona Elspeth
**Age:** 39
**Address:** 12 Rowan House, Ashen Row, Badger's Haze
**Occupation:** Licensed Magical Healer/Lecturer in Empathic Studies
**Magical specialty:** Empathic healing
**Next of kin:** None and unmarried. No children.

**Case summary**

The body was discovered on October

20, 2001, at approximately 8:30 a.m. by Lavender Quell in the conservatory of the victim's home. The victim was found collapsed in a chair, clutching an ornate silver brooch (identified as The Heart of the Healer.) There was no visible external trauma, and preliminary readings note a residual surge of magical energy prior to death. Autopsy pending. To be conducted by Doctor Thelma Greaves.

**Evidence collected**

Silver brooch with ruby heart (The Heart of the Healer), enchanted, with active runes (Crispin Vance's signature confirmed.)
Three wilted hellebore blooms, scattered on the floor near the chair.
Magical residue: empathic echo suggesting sudden pain or fear (to be confirmed.)

**Timeline**

**October 19, 2001**
9:00 a.m. The victim lectured at Badger's Haze Academy all day
5:15 p.m. Sighted at Apothecary Guildhall
6:30 p.m. Globe call logged to Dr. Thelma Greaves

9:45 p.m. Last confirmed alive (neighbor saw lights on and heard raised voices)
8:30 a.m. Body discovered by Lavender Quell

**Persons of interest (primary suspects)**

**Lavender Quell (32):** Potion mistress and friend.
**Crispin Vance (37):** Jewelry maker, confirmed creator of the Heart of the Healer, and worked closely with the victim.
**Delphine Noxley (29):** Local healer, although she recently stopped practicing due to the victim's recommendation.
**Hester Gull (31):** Animist. Known locally as an eccentric hermit.
**Minnie (age unknown):** Victim's cat familiar. Missing since being discovered and questioned at the scene.

# Chapter 3

"Angel Force appears not to have been so thorough this time around. Standards were already slipping." I sat in front of the snow globe, peering at Sage, whose image was fuzzy. I couldn't decide if it was because she'd recently had a bath or if the connection was dubious.

"What does the autopsy say?" Sage asked.

"I couldn't find one."

"All strange deaths get a slice and dice. Why wasn't it done?"

"Unknown. Maybe the paperwork got lost. The cause of death is woolly, though."

"There's a decent suspect list," Sage said. "Is there a record of which suspect Angel Force considered the killer?"

I shook my head. "I've looked through the files several times, and it's almost as if they grew bored with investigating and decided it would be simpler to close the case and move on. Most likely to a plate of brownies and a cup of coffee."

"Don't be such a cynic. Most of the angels here do a decent job," Sage said.

"I have a touch of bias," I admitted, "but you can hardly blame me. Still banished here after doing such incredible work. Not even a thank you note."

"Your bunch of flowers and box of chocolates are on their way, once the decision has passed approval through the various committees," Sage said. "I did some reading about that Heart of the Healers while digesting my second dinner. It's powerful jewelry, and not something you want to mess around with if your own powers are so limited. Need I remind you, yours are?"

I forced a few magical sparkles out of one paw pad. "I have power! It's strange to use borrowed magic, though. And I don't know how long it'll stick around, so don't want to get used to it in case it's taken away."

"Or you're too lazy to practice," Sage said. "Let's pick a simpler case. One where the jewelry doesn't hex you to death."

"It got the nickname the hexed heart because it was found with Dr. Wren's body. It could be a coincidence that it was there."

"It got that nickname because there's something wrong with it."

"This case called to me," I said. "Dr. Wren must have helped so many people during her career. With her enhanced empathic abilities, she'd have soothed many a troubled soul. She deserves justice."

Sage huffed out a breath. "If you're doing this, I'd better stick around and make sure you don't get yourself killed."

"Your support is touching," I said. "Which suspect shall we start with? That's assuming they're all alive."

"The case is over twenty years old," Sage said. "It's possible some will have left or died. You may have to sneak into the cemetery and chat with the corpses."

"I'll never get through the gates! Not with the village's ever-efficient, terrifying guardian stalking around."

"Let's make a plan. Step one, we find out which suspects are still around to question," Sage said.

"I've got a better idea," I said. "It's almost stopped raining, so I'm willing to venture outside. I'll speak to Dr. Greaves. She was in charge of Iona's autopsy, so she could still have a copy of the autopsy report."

"Is she still in Badger's Haze?"

"Yes, I've heard her spoken about, although she's retired," I said. "She lives on the edge of the village."

"As far away from trouble as possible," Sage said. "I don't blame her. She sees the sharp end of what happens when a coroner gets involved."

"I'll go now before it gets too dark."

"Be careful out there," Sage said. "You've still got a mostly hostile crowd watching your every move."

"I'll stick to the shadows, which is no hard task in this murky place. I'll go straight to Dr. Greaves's house and have an intelligent conversation. I miss those."

"Hey! What do you think we've been doing?"

"Sorry, I missed that. The snow globe is malfunctioning again." I snickered to myself. "I'll catch up with you later."

I smiled as I left Sage grumbling and hurried to the creaky main door. As I eased it open, I grimaced. The rain had held off for a full five minutes, but a freezing mist dampened my fur as I dashed along.

When I got out of here—and I would get out—I intended to spend at least a month on a tropical island, doing nothing but having my toe beans massaged and drinking milk-based cocktails with umbrellas and prawns stuck on the side of the glass. And of course, Zandra would be with me. We needed time to catch up after being yanked apart so cruelly.

I did my best to avoid the mud and deep puddles, taking the back roads for fifteen minutes to get to the edge of the village, speeding up when I spotted a welcoming glow of light at my destination.

Dr. Greaves lived in an adorable cottage, its honey-stone walls wrapped in a tangle of ivy and climbing roses. A thatched roof dipped low over leaded windows, their panes glinting like watchful eyes. Smoke curled lazily from the chimney, and a white gate sagged just enough to creak when opened, guarding a tiny front garden where lavender, foxgloves, and herbs grew.

I was heading along the overgrown front path when a gruff-faced gnome holding a pointed stick accosted me.

He bared his little teeth. "She's not selling whatever you're buying."

"Greetings! I'm selling nothing. I simply seek information." I attempted to step around the chonky chap, but he rudely jabbed me in the side with his stick.

I hissed at him. "I appreciate that you want to protect your owner, but—"

"Nobody owns me or my friends. We're free spirits, and Thelma lets us live here. We look after her garden and see off troublemakers like you."

I glanced around, suddenly aware that a dozen pairs of eyes were glaring at me from the undergrowth. They most likely had pointy sticks, too.

"I'm sure you do an excellent job," I said. "But as I already told you, I'm here for information, not to cause trouble, and not to sell anything. It's most important. It's about a murder."

"Who have you murdered?" The gnome stepped menacingly toward me.

"I'm tempted to murder you if you don't let me past," I said. "Dr. Greaves conducted an autopsy some years back on Dr. Iona Wren. I need to find out what the autopsy revealed."

"She's retired. She doesn't do that anymore," the gnome said. "Move along unless you want to lose that pretty tail of yours."

I wrapped my tail firmly around my front paws and stepped on it. My tail had been taken once before, and I'd make sure that never happened again.

"What's going on out here?" A thin-faced woman with a large pair of dark-rimmed spectacles looked out the front window, which she'd cracked open an inch.

"This fluffy is bothering us," the gnome said. "She's talking about murder. She wants to ask you questions about an autopsy. I told her you don't do that anymore."

Dr. Greaves peered over the top of her glasses at me. "I know you. Well, I know of you. You're that cat who lives in the library. The one the angels sent here for misbehaving."

"Greetings! I'm Juno, and I have a temporary base in the library. But being sent here was a mistake. One Angel Force is rectifying, though you know how slowly the wheels of law enforcement turn." I forced a laugh. "While I'm here, I'm investigating the cold cases too difficult for the angels to solve, and I wanted to speak to you about the autopsy you did on Dr. Iona Wren. Do you remember that case?"

"Shall I chase her off?" the gnome asked. "I'll give her a stick poke and send her on her way."

Dr. Greaves drew in a slow breath and pushed her glasses up her nose. "There's no need. I remember the case. I always wanted to know what happened to Iona. It was a strange death, and I thought about it for many months after the angels closed the case." She gestured me closer. "Come inside, Juno. Don't mind the gnomes. They're meaner than they look, although make sure not to tread on their mushrooms."

"I'll be sure not to touch them. I have a healthy respect for fungi." I dodged past the glaring gnome and his pointy stick and dashed to the door Dr. Greaves had opened for me.

I stepped inside a cluttered hallway, and Dr. Greaves showed me into an equally chaotic living room with piles of paper and books and several plates and cups lying scattered around. She made no apology for the mess, simply cleared a space on a chair and gestured for me to sit.

I nodded my thanks and hopped up onto the comfortable spot.

Dr. Greaves was a sprightly-looking sixty-year-old. Her wild gray curls were unbrushed, her cardigan misbuttoned, and she wore different-colored socks.

She'd just settled into a seat when there was a shrill whistle from the kitchen, causing her to leap up. "I'll be back in a moment. I must add the bramble to the hellebore, or a whole day of work will have been for nothing."

I followed her into the kitchen, which was more like a miniature laboratory than a place for baking delicious pies. "Is this what you do in your retirement?"

She didn't glance up from her frantic stirring and checking. "I can't seem to keep away from the dead. Well, I mean, I want to help the dead. You know how our dead are. They don't like to stay dead for long. It's all that pent-up magic pinging around. I volunteer at the cemetery to keep things under control. I also do a weekly walkthrough of the abandoned cemetery. You never know what might peek out."

"What do you do to help the dead? Rebury them?"

Dr. Greaves huffed out a laugh. "I work on finding a stabilizer for their magic. This is my third batch this month. It seems to hold, but then a pesky corpse will rise, and off we go again. Mind you, I'd say it's not just the pent-up magic that causes the problem. All of Badger's Haze is crumbling. Not that anyone cares. Those of us stuck living here do the best we can, but it feels like we're losing."

"Badger's Haze exudes a rough charm," I said.

"That's one way of describing it. I decided in my retirement to help the dead rest a little more easily, so those of us still living don't find corpses wandering up our front paths and bothering our gnomes." She finally glanced at me, and a wry smile crossed her face. "You must think I'm eccentric."

"I think it's fascinating," I said. "And I have a deep respect for cemetery guardian magic. In your former career, you must have crossed paths with one or two of them. They can be... spiky. I've met Morticia."

Dr. Greaves let out a bark of laughter. "When you get past the hissing and snarling, she's enthralling company."

"She must be," I said. "Did Morticia bury Iona in her cemetery, or is Iona's body in the abandoned cemetery? I'm unsure when that was closed."

"Neither option was possible." Dr. Greaves finally seemed satisfied with her work and gestured for us to go back to the living room, where she perched on the edge of her chair. "Iona's body turned to ash."

I jerked back. "Ash! How did that happen?"

"Cause unknown. I never had a chance to conduct a full autopsy. I ran some preliminaries and did a first sweep, if you like, but when I went back the next day to finish, there was a pile of ash where her body should have been. It was as if she were a vampire. Which, of course, she wasn't." Dr. Greaves let out a sigh. "Iona was a powerful healer and used empathic medicine and magic. Her abilities were extraordinary. She was an incredibly strong magic user."

"That makes sense," I said. "I found no autopsy in the case file."

Dr. Greaves' strident eyebrows flashed up. "You have access to the cold case files for Badger's Haze?"

"They're stored in the library," I said. "I like to keep myself busy too."

"An excellent idea. Idle magical hands—or paws—cause trouble." She cocked her head. "Although your magic has an interesting flavor. It feels like someone I used to know."

"Getting back to Iona," I said swiftly. "Do you have any information about her autopsy that I can read? It could be useful in my investigation."

"I keep copies of all my cases. It's not strictly allowed, but I like to reference the work I've conducted. It helps give me context sometimes. Wait here. I'll be back in a few moments." She stood, then paused. "Touch nothing. I have a chaotic order in here, and I'll know if something has been moved."

I mooched around the living room, peering at papers but making sure my paws made no contact. I also glanced out at the gnomes to find them guarding the house. Grumpy little pokers.

"Here we are." Dr. Greaves returned a few moments later with a file in her hand. She set it down on the floor for me and flipped open the pages.

I peered at the small, dense text and frowned. This would take me time to digest. Dr. Greaves appeared to use ten words when two would do. "Were you close to Iona?"

"We were more professionally close than friends," Dr. Greaves said. "Although I spoke to her on the day she died. It played on my mind for some time because she seemed worried about her work with the brooch. Do you know about that?"

"Yes. The Heart of the Healer," I said. "What were her concerns about it?"

"It wasn't called that following Iona's demise. People started using the name the hexed heart, and it stuck." Dr. Greaves shuffled the pages of the file. "Iona wouldn't say what troubled her, but I heard worry in her voice. We talked not long before she died."

"You were with her that night?"

"No. I was a workaholic, and I probably still am, even though I'm retired," Dr. Greaves said. "You'd often find me working on a body or writing up a report well into the early hours. I'd fallen asleep at my desk that night, but I woke to the terrible news about what had happened to Iona. My assistant was in floods of tears, saying she couldn't believe it."

"It must have been a shock for both of you," I said.

"It was," Dr. Greaves replied. "We both worked with people, though in different ways. Iona healed the living, but my work was just as important. I gave the dead the respect owed to them. Just because you die, it doesn't mean you should be treated like a lump of meat. And anyone who visits the cemetery knows our magic lives on."

"It's certainly the case with the Badger's Haze cemetery."

Dr. Greaves nodded. "We're all energy. And energy cannot be destroyed. It simply transforms. Wander around those headstones and you see that transformation with your own eyes."

"It's an extraordinary place," I said, not dwelling on my own brushes with death whenever I went near that hallowed ground. "Do you know of anyone who had a problem with Iona?"

Dr. Greaves closed her eyes, her forehead wrinkling as if dredging old memories. "There were people in the village who weren't fond of her. Delphine Noxley comes to mind. She lost her license to practice because Iona spoke out against her."

"What did she say?" I asked.

"That Delphine was incompetent. They often argued about it. Delphine is... a prickly individual. But if memory serves, Angel Force questioned her and found nothing to suggest a connection to Iona's murder."

"I have her name in the case file," I said. "Does Delphine still live in the village?"

"She's still here. Very much a presence, shall we say." Dr. Greaves's smile was sardonic.

"What about the other suspects Angel Force identified?" I asked.

"You'll have to remind me of the names," Dr. Greaves said.

"Lavender Quell."

"Oh, yes. She's still here."

"Crispin Vance," I said. "He made the brooch that killed Iona."

"Him!" Dr. Greaves pulled a face as if she'd just sucked on a lemon. "I can't see him ever leaving. His family established itself here hundreds of years ago, and even though there's nothing much to speak of in Badger's Haze these days, the place is in his blood. That's what he tells people, anyway. He's still practicing as a jewelry maker."

"You don't like him?"

"I... I don't trust him. He barely has any customers, but he always has money. I have no proof, but he doesn't run a legitimate business."

"Thank you. That's useful. What about Hester Gull?"

Dr. Greaves pulled another face. "As long as Hester's ravens live here, she'll be here. She has a flock of birds she cares for. We all call her the Raven Whisperer. But be careful around Hester. She has power when controlling animals. She may use it on you if she doesn't like the look of you."

"I'm above being controlled by spells." I stopped myself. In the past, that statement would have held true, but now, I could probably be manipulated if someone waved a bag of catnip-scented treats under my booping snooter.

"Even so, most of us keep away from her because her eccentricities lead to spitefulness. You'll find her trekking around in the trees, and she's often lurking about the forbidden herb garden."

"There's a forbidden herb garden in the village?" I asked.

"It's a well-kept local secret." Dr. Greaves leaned closer. "Rare and particularly dangerous herbs grow in a specific area. It's like a miniature poison cemetery. You only go in there if you want something you really shouldn't be using."

"I'll visit and see if I can find Hester," I said. "What about Iona's familiar, Minnie?"

"Oh, that poor little thing." Dr. Greaves's expression fell. "I hope she found peace before she passed."

"Minnie is dead?"

"Well, I assume so," Dr. Greaves said. "A familiar doesn't thrive when its bonded magic user dies. Minnie was there when it happened. It must have been such a shock to her system. Minnie was never the strongest cat, and after her injury, where she lost the sight in one eye, well... we never thought she was strong enough to be Iona's familiar, but they carried on."

"Did you see Minnie after Iona died?"

"Only briefly when I went to assist with the body removal. She sat shivering under a chair in the room where Iona had been killed. Then Minnie vanished. I assumed she crawled into a hole and lay down to die," Dr. Greaves said. "Angel Force did a brief interview with her, then searched for her for days with more questions, but never found her."

"That's a tragedy." I swallowed against the tight feeling in my throat. "Most familiars pine away swiftly when the bond dies."

"Yes. Your bonds are extraordinary, but they come with a price." Dr. Greaves glanced around the room. "It's why I never sought one. I wouldn't bother trying to find Minnie. That would be a waste of effort."

"Thank you. I appreciate all the information," I said. "Could I take the autopsy paperwork? I'd like to look at the details and see if it leads me anywhere."

"Be my guest, but there's not much information in there. And I want it back." Dr. Greaves touched my paw. "I'd consider it a personal favor if you discovered what happened to Iona. It was a tragedy. She was taken too soon. She helped so many, and she could have helped many more if her life hadn't been cut tragically short."

"That's my plan. And I'm happy to keep you informed."

"Let me roll up the papers and tie them so you don't lose any pages on your way home."

I appreciated Dr. Greaves's help, and once the autopsy report was secured to my back with a long piece of string tied around my middle, she showed me to the front door.

"Good luck. You'd better run when you leave," Dr. Greaves said. "You don't want to be stabbed by a gnome just as you're getting going."

I couldn't tell if she was joking, so after a brief goodbye, I checked the path was clear of stabby, mean-tempered gnomes, and bolted.

# Chapter 4

"I'll share you the pain of having to read through Dr. Greaves's autopsy notes," I said. "She doesn't speak like she writes."

"What's wrong with it?" Sage's nose almost brushed the snow globe glass, making her look all booping snooter and no ears.

"It's dull. And dense. I fell asleep twice wading through the jargon."

"Let me see some of it," Sage said. "I'm used to stuffy old books."

"That would be too cruel."

"Maybe I'm smarter than you."

"I think you mean grumpier."

Sage snorted. "Send it over."

"I'll send one section. But don't say I didn't warn you." I tinkered with the snow globe until it stopped smoking and sent through the report.

*Based on rigor onset and ambient room temperature (46°F at time of body discovery), the estimated time of death is between 21:30 and 23:00 hours.*

*This estimation was subsequently adjusted to 22:45 ± 15 minutes to account for digestion variances in empathic healers, whose metabolic rates are irregular (see Appendix F: Healer Metabolic Variations, 23pp). Therefore, the official time of death was certified at 22:45 hours.*

*This conclusion is consistent with coroner best practice standards and requires no further scrutiny.*

"Are you asleep yet?" I asked after waiting a minute for Sage to digest the dullness.

"I thought Dr. Greaves only did an initial look at the body. It says here there are twenty-three pages of notes."

"It's mainly references to other reports or journals. Dr. Greaves planned on conducting the full autopsy the next day, but by then, all that was left of Iona was a pile of ash."

"And Iona definitely wasn't a vampire? Are we sure about that?" Sage asked. "Maybe she had some vampire in her ancestry and something snuck through."

"Angel Force ran a full family background check. There wasn't a drop of vampire in there," I said. "Iona was a powerful healing witch, not a vampire."

Sage grunted. "So, what turned her to ash?"

"Someone with power," I said.

"And someone who wanted to hide the evidence before the autopsy happened because it would have revealed their involvement."

I nodded. "Before Badger's Haze became a magical backwater full of disgruntled grumps, the people living here had access to magic that would have turned Iona into ash."

"Maybe some of them still do, but they got good at hiding it."

"We need to look at who was closest to our victim," I said. "Now I've spoken to Dr. Greaves, we have somewhere to go. And other than the deceased familiar, Minnie, they're all still living here, so I can speak to them."

"It's a pity Minnie didn't make it," Sage said. "Especially since she was at the crime scene. She would have seen it all. She could have pointed a paw directly at her witch's killer and solved this mystery."

"Minnie must have been too broken to carry on," I said. "I'd be the same if I ever lost Zandra for good."

"The same goes for me and Vorana. She's the only reason I keep going. She's my world."

"That's an unhelpful way to look at things," I said.

"What do you mean?"

"If you say another person is your world, it places a weight upon their shoulders. It's like when people say their children are their entire world. What does that do to the poor children, trying to find their way through a twisty, magical existence with that added burden of responsibility?"

Sage cocked her head. "Huh. I'd never thought of that. Maybe Vorana is my moon, then. Would that work? The moon is crucial for lots of spells, but we can still do magic without it."

"You need to find interests other than your witch."

"Like solving crime and annoying Angel Force. That worked out so well for you."

I ignored her jab. "Give Vorana space."

"Yuck. I hate that thought. If my space isn't full of Vorana, then I'm unsettled."

"I get it." I sighed. A bonded pair thrived off each other's magic and gave each other strength. It was another reason I needed to get back to Zandra. She was vulnerable without me. I should try that angle with Angel Force, get them to see sense. Although they had little of that rattling around in their feather-filled brains.

Sage sat forward, her booping snooter filling the snow globe so I could barely see her. "Are you in that library alone?"

"Unless you count the ghosts, I'm always alone here," I said, with a deliberately mournful lilt to my voice.

"I saw movement behind you."

I glanced over my shoulder. "It's probably another library specter. They've been restless recently."

"It looked too solid to be a ghost," Sage said.

"I can't think who else it would be," I said. "I don't get visitors. I was hoping to form a friendship with Roland after we dug him up and brought him back from the brink of death, but he's vanished."

"You know who your real friends are when you get on the wrong side of Angel Force and get sent to a hexed village where everyone hates you," Sage said.

"Yes. You're my nearest, dearest, and only friend," I said. "And even you don't visit."

She closed one eye and then the other. "There's definitely something moving between the book stacks in the far corner of that room."

I was about to turn when a book being knocked off a shelf made me freeze.

"Which side do you see movement?" I whispered.

"I'll tell you when to look over your right shoulder," Sage replied. "Whatever it is, it's small and dark. It has four legs."

"You're sure it's not a ghost?" I asked. "I haven't met all of them, and there was talk of a ghostly dog lurking somewhere on the top level. I've kept away. Not all dogs admire our fine features."

"Wait for it... wait for it," Sage murmured. "Now!"

I whirled around just in time to see a long, dark, skinny tail disappear from view. "Uh oh. I'm used to seeing the ghosts drifting around, but that was too small to be a regular ghost." I scanned the room, vigilant for movement.

"You've got an intruder," Sage said.

"Then it's a good job I have magic to see them off." I sparked a spell on my paws. It flickered for a few seconds, uncertain it wanted to behave, but it remained with me.

"You're still not adept at using that magic," Sage said. "Find a weapon to take with you."

"I'm not beating a stranger around the head just because they've sought refuge in the library," I said.

"You need to do it to them before they do it to you."

"Your cynicism is showing." I kept searching but saw no small four-legged critters with a tail.

"And your confidence is bubbling over like a witch's cauldron," Sage said. "Lock yourself in a cupboard. Maybe they'll be gone by morning."

There was another soft thud as a book hit the floor.

"It sounds as if they're looking for something," I whispered. "I'm going to see what they're after."

"And get yourself killed!" Sage hissed. "This is the wrong time to die. You're just getting stuck into another cold case."

"I'll be careful. Don't go anywhere."

"As if I would. I want to make sure you don't get yourself into too much of a mess."

"You should talk. You've got butter smeared on your chest."

Sage attempted to look at her own chest and failed. "It's hollandaise sauce. Vorana was feeling fancy when she made food earlier."

I was only half listening, already creeping away from the snow globe, keeping my belly low to the floor. I had a trickle of magic back, but it was nowhere near what I was used to, so I had to be cautious. But I needed to know who hid in my library. Well, it wasn't my library, but my temporary home, and I had to make sure it was safe. It would be impossible to have comfy naps if something lurked in the shadows.

Were there any helpful library ghosts about? Nope. As usual, they were off doing something eccentric and scholarly, most likely throwing quills and acting out a scene from *Macbeth.*

My paws barely made a sound as I crept past book stacks. I was on the right path, given that several books had been pushed from the shelf and not returned. As I inched along, soft panting reached my ears. Whoever was lurking about was in distress.

I rounded the corner and stopped. A triangular stack of books blocked the way. It looked like someone had made a book tent. There was even a small opening at the front to get in and out.

"Greetings. Is anyone in there?" I asked. "You have nothing to fear. I don't mind you being here, but I would like to know who's sharing this space with me."

There was no reply. Was the panting coming from behind the book tent?

I walked all around it and sniffed close to the opening. A bedraggled paw shot out, claws extended, and raked down my perfect booping snooter.

I yelped and threw myself back, rolling nose over tail until I landed on my belly. My paw swiped several times over the injury, then growled when my white fur became smeared with blood.

"That's no way to behave if you expect to stay here." I hissed fiercely at the dark opening leading into the book tent. "Show yourself before I knock these books on your head and crush you."

A pitiful meow echoed out of the darkness.

It was a cat! Or at least something pretending to be a cat.

I forced out a basic healing spell after a few false starts, which I wiped over the injury on my booping snooter. It wouldn't do a perfect job, but at least it took away the sting.

"I won't tell you again. Come out, or down those books go," I snarled.

There was a shuffling from inside the book tent, and a few seconds later, a bedraggled-looking black-and-white head poked out. One sad green eye looked at me. The other was cloudy and stared at nothing.

I froze, breath catching in my throat. It couldn't be, could it? "Are you Minnie?"

# Chapter 5

Minnie's ears flattened, and in the next heartbeat, she bolted out of the book tent, sending an avalanche of books tumbling in all directions.

"Running only makes you look guilty!" I launched after her.

She tore down the nearest aisle, scattering books with every swipe of her paws. A heavy tome hit the floor with a crack. Minnie tripped over it, rolled nose over tail, then sprang back up with surprising speed for someone so bedraggled.

I charged after her. A fizz of magic sparked at my paw pads, and I flung it forward. The spell flared, dazzlingly bright, but it fizzled into nothing but a puff of glitter that rained down on my head.

The library ghosts drifted in, muttering Shakespearean insults at one another. One spun dramatically, swooped low, and knocked a row of books down just as Minnie tried to dart past. She squealed, crashed into the pile, and vanished under a small avalanche of paperbacks.

"Cry havoc, and let slip the cats of war!" one ghost bellowed, hurling a phantom quill at my tail.

"Don't fight me, you buffoon! I'm the good cat!" I hissed, shook it off, and leaped over the book pile.

Minnie shot out from the other side like a rocket, fur bristling, paws scrabbling wildly as she tried to find her footing. She skidded around a corner, clipped a chair leg, and somersaulted across the carpet.

By the time I caught up, she was staggering to her paws again, panting hard, her eyes wide.

Another burst of magic sparked from me. This time it took the shape of a glowing net that hung in the air for half a glorious second before drooping like a damp dishcloth. Minnie dashed right through it, trailing shreds of light.

I gathered myself, sprang, and collided with her just as she scrambled past the snow globe. We tumbled together, paws and tails flailing. She wriggled, hissed, and tried to twist free, but I slammed my weight down and pinned her to the floor.

Minnie froze, her chest heaving, one cloudy eye staring at me, the other burning bright green. Slowly, the fight bled out of her.

She sagged beneath me with a long, broken sigh. "Fine. You win."

The snow globe flickered beside us, Sage's face pressed so close to the glass I could see her whiskers flatten against it. "Hey! Is that Minnie?"

"I believe so. The not so dead familiar," I said.

"I may as well be dead." Minnie closed her eyes and exposed her throat.

"What are you doing?" I asked.

"Letting you take the killing blow. Do it. Put me out of my misery."

I stepped back.

Minnie opened one eye. "Why am I not dead?"

"Because I want to ask you some questions. I'm Juno, and this is Sage."

"Yeah. I want to ask if you killed Iona?" Sage said.

"Everyone thinks I did." Minnie stayed on her back, her legs in the air, showing off the white socks on her front paws. "But I didn't. Why would I? She was my witch. We protect our witches. We don't harm them."

"Perhaps something went wrong with your magic," Sage said. "You made a mistake, and your witch died."

"I was as powerful as Iona." Minnie opened her other eye and waggled her paws in the air. "We chose each other because our powers blended so perfectly. Why would I want to lose that?"

"Get up," I said.

"I don't have the strength. I haven't eaten in days. Leave me here to wither."

"Wait there," I ordered.

"Why wait? Do it. End this torment."

"She's dramatic," Sage muttered.

"I'll get you some food. Just no running off." I dashed to my pitiful stash of supplies and bit off a large chunk of tinned ham. Carrying it back to Minnie, I dropped it by her nose.

Minnie threw herself at the food and gulped it down, barely chewing.

I dragged back the rest of the tin, and she polished it off in less than thirty seconds.

"I'm sorry about what happened to your witch," I said.

Minnie licked her face clean. "So am I."

"Everyone thought you had died," Sage said.

"That's what I wanted them to believe." Minnie sniffed inside the empty tin of ham. "Otherwise, I'd be behind bars and charged with her murder."

"Is that because you did it?" Sage asked.

Minnie let out a pitiful howl and slashed pointlessly at the snow globe.

"That's a no, I take it?" I asked.

"I've already told you. My job was to protect Iona."

"With great power comes great responsibility," I said. "I've known a few spells go wrong. They put my witch at risk."

"Where is your witch?" Minnie glanced around the library.

"It's a long story," I said with a sigh.

"Angel Force banished Juno here," Sage explained. "She's been separated from her witch, Zandra Crypt."

"Which is a tragedy," I replied. "And one I'm fixing, which is why I need to solve Iona's murder."

"I... I don't get it," Minnie said.

"Juno thinks that if she solves enough cold cases, Angel Force will take pity on her and let her leave Badger's Haze," Sage said.

Minnie scrunched up her nose. "No one leaves Badger's Haze. I'd have left if I could, but we're all tethered here. Even people who get out come back. Did you know there's a curse on this village?"

"I thought it was a hex," Sage said.

"Hex, spell, troublesome potion poured into the water well," Minnie said. "It's all the same thing. We're trapped in this desolate misery for eternity. And I have to do it without Iona by my side."

"You'd get comfort if you solved what happened to her," I said. "You were there when she died?"

Minnie sighed shakily. "I was under the chair."

"So, you saw what happened?" Sage asked.

"I... I might have done, but my memories are confused. When Iona was attacked, the hexed heart—that evil brooch she was obsessed with—did something strange."

"What did it do?" I asked.

"Light flared out of it. It covered everything in the room, including me. I couldn't see, but I also couldn't move or think straight. I dragged myself under a chair, but the power within that jewelry was too intense. I blacked out and only came to when someone came into the room."

"What about before Iona was attacked?" I asked. "Did anyone visit her?"

Minnie shook her head. "That whole evening is a blur. I remember earlier in the day, she was focused. She said she'd had a breakthrough with the brooch and wanted to work on it for the rest of the day. I knew what that meant."

"What did she mean?" I asked.

"Iona was obsessed with empathic magic. She always wanted to help people with their troubles. The world is a troubled place, and people struggle. Iona would absorb their energy and fix them."

"Did you feel that too?" I asked.

"To some degree, but not as acutely as Iona." Minnie tipped back her head and howled at the ceiling.

"What are you doing?" Sage asked. "Are you in pain?"

"It's a grief cry. I sometimes do it when I'm full of rage, too," Minnie said. "Iona would go into the forest and howl at the moon like a wild thing. She said it was good to let out pent-up emotions with a good scream or two. She needed to do it to dispel all the twisted, troubled emotions she'd take on when working with patients."

"I'll have to try that," I said. "You remember nothing about that evening?"

"I really don't. Of course, if I knew who had murdered Iona, I'd have gone after them and torn them to shreds, but it's all so hazy."

"Where have you been all this time?" Sage asked. "After Angel Force came on the scene, you disappeared."

"I've been living here."

"In the library?" I asked.

"No. I have no home anymore. I live wherever I can find that's not too damp or dangerous," Minnie said.

"What about Iona's home?" Sage asked. "You can't get inside?"

"I never go back there. There are too many sad memories," Minnie said.

"Or you don't want to go back there because you might get arrested," I said.

Minnie scowled at the floor. "I knew Angel Force would want to question me again, and I couldn't handle it. When they arrived with Dr. Greaves and took Iona away, a piece of me was destroyed. I've never found it again."

"You've been in hiding all this time?" I asked.

"There are places to go if you know where to look," Minnie said.

"Who do you think did this?" I asked. "You must have a suspect in mind."

"Iona's murder has to be connected to Crispin," Minnie said with a decisive nod. "He coveted the hexed heart. Did you know he made it?"

"He's on the list to speak to," I said. "Why would he want Iona dead?"

"Because she had a better bond with the brooch than he did. He was jealous. He crafted that piece of jewelry, so it should have had a natural resonance with him, but Iona was much more powerful," Minnie said. "There are some men who don't like women with power and influence. Crispin is one of them."

"Did you never confront him?" Sage asked. "If anyone went after my witch, I'd destroy them, then dig up the body, set it on fire, and shoot it into the air. Anything that was left, I'd trample it to dust. Then I'd collect that dust, roll it in honey badger excrement, and throw it into a volcano. And then—"

"We get the idea, Sage," I said. "You love Vorana and you'd seek the worst revenge."

"It sounds like the best revenge," Minnie said.

"All I'm saying is, if Minnie knows for sure Crispin is the killer, why hasn't she gotten her revenge?" Sage asked.

"My power has faded," Minnie said. "When Iona died, it felt as if someone flicked a switch inside me. I used to feel what other people felt and help them if they were troubled, just like Iona. But that's all gone. I'm now just a big ball of furry numbness."

"Other than the rage and the grief screaming," Sage said.

"That comes in short bursts, and it's rarely helpful," Minnie said. "I'm useless. And I grow weaker all the time."

"But you still have your ear to the ground," I said. "You came out of hiding to find me, didn't you?"

Minnie nodded. "I heard from the gnomes that someone was asking questions about Iona's murder, and I wanted to find out why."

"Because you're worried we may find evidence pointing to you?" Sage asked.

Minnie swatted at the snow globe and hissed. "I need to find out what happened. I must learn the truth so I can rest in peace. Otherwise, I'll be dragging this useless carcass of mine around forever, never able to settle because of what happened, and because I failed to protect my witch."

"I could do with some help," I said. "You know Badger's Haze better than I do, so people may open up to you."

"The locals don't talk to each other, let alone a stranger," Minnie said. "And I'm not sure how helpful I'll be. They think I'm spooky."

"Is it because of the rage and grief screaming?" Sage asked.

"No! It's because of my eye. I lost sight in one eye protecting Iona from an unstable Hexen beast. Iona tried every spell she could think of to get back my sight, but I ended up with a haunted-looking eyeball."

"You could try an eye patch," I said. "But the eye doesn't offend me. It makes you look quirky."

Minnie huffed out a breath. "Quirky to you is spooky to everyone else."

"I like it," Sage said. "Adds character."

Minnie shrugged but sat up straighter. "Thanks. And I'll help. You're the only ones who have shown any interest in figuring out what happened to Iona. I can't even remember the last time anyone so much as spoke her name."

"Juno, could I have a quiet word?" Sage asked.

"There's another tin of ham in that box," I said to Minnie, gesturing to the other side of the room. "Grab it while I talk to Sage."

"I might go back and rebuild my book tent," Minnie said. "With the tinned ham, of course. That was tasty." She walked away but then stopped and looked back at me. "I can trust you, can't I?"

"I'll do my very best to find out what happened to your witch," I said. "It's in both of our interests to solve this mystery."

Minnie tipped back her head, howled again, then wandered off to snaffle my ham.

"You can't trust her," Sage whispered.

"Shush. Minnie might hear you," I said.

"She's a suspect in this murder investigation. Don't believe what she tells you. She's unstable."

"So would you be if something destroyed Vorana and then turned her into ash," I said.

"She's been hiding from Angel Force for a good reason," Sage replied. "Minnie had the perfect opportunity to commit the crime, since she was always with Iona."

"That cat is broken beyond repair and full of grief and pain," I said.

"Or full of guilt, and wanting to make sure we find no evidence that lands her behind bars."

"What's Minnie's motive?" I asked.

"Familiar bonds fracture," Sage said. "And it sounds like Iona was obsessed with the hexed heart. Minnie could have gotten jealous and lashed out. She might have felt abandoned by her witch and wanted the focus back on her."

I sat back and considered the possibilities, keeping one ear on Minnie, who noisily munched the tinned ham, hidden behind a bookshelf. "She was at the murder scene, so I won't completely discount her from the suspect list."

"You need to lock her up! Make sure she doesn't turn you to ash, too," Sage said.

"Keep your friends close and your enemies closer. If I enlist Minnie's help, then I can watch what she does. Anything strange, and I'll look into it. And if I discover her attempting to misdirect me or tamper with evidence, then it'll be proof she's hiding her guilt."

"That's if you live long enough," Sage said. "Don't get cocky just because you've got a little magic running through those paws again."

"My murder mittens are perfectly primed for anything Minnie throws at me." I jumped as the empty tin of ham hit the back of my head.

Sage laughed. "You weren't prepared for that."

I glowered at the tin. "Minnie, was that you?"

She poked her head around the side of a bookshelf. "Was that me what?"

Two ghosts swooped past, cackling and pointing at me. Wretched spirits.

"Nothing. Go back to your book tent." I turned to Sage. "Make yourself useful and review Crispin's interview with Angel Force. Sending it through now."

**Case File:** #2001-1020
**Subject:** Vance, Crispin
**Interviewer:** Angel Sarah
**Location:** Vance Jewelry Studio, 8 Glint Alley, Badger's Haze

**ANGEL SARAH:** Please state your full name and magical occupation for the record.

**VANCE:** Crispin Elliot Vance. Enchanted jeweler, third generation. Specializing in magically attuned heirlooms and symbolic objects.

**ANGEL SARAH:** What was your relationship to the victim, Dr. Iona Wren?

**VANCE:** We worked together, on and off, for decades. She trusted my work. I understand the emotional resonance of an object, not just the sparkle.

**ANGEL SARAH:** Was it just a professional relationship?

**VANCE:** We weren't close in the social sense. Iona wasn't much for dinner parties, but there was mutual respect. She was one of the strongest magic users I've ever met. Empathic healing is no joke. She could anchor someone's grief in objects and help them breathe again.

**ANGEL SARAH:** Were you surprised to learn of her death?

**VANCE:** Shocked. Completely. I mean, I didn't believe it at first. I thought it was some sick error. Iona didn't make magical mistakes. If she had an object that was cursed, she would have known. She was too careful.

**ANGEL SARAH:** Dr. Wren was found holding a brooch. Do you know anything about that?

**VANCE:** Everyone knows about the Heart of the Healer, but I thought she'd archived it years ago. It's an old piece, practically a relic. What did it do to her?

**ANGEL SARAH:** She died.

**VANCE:** I... sure. I know that. Was it quick? Was she alone? I can't figure out how it went wrong.

**ANGEL SARAH:** The specifics are under investigation.

**VANCE:** Iona must have known

something was off with the magic. Unless... unless someone altered the enchantments. Can you tell me what was found with her? Any spell work? Signs of interference?

**ANGEL SARAH:** The scene contained a partially drawn ritual circle and residual traces of alignment magic. Does that mean anything to you?

**VANCE:** Oh! Well, it sounds like Iona was experimenting again. She was obsessed with empathy-channeled alignment work, believing it healed deep trauma. I thought it was too unstable. I told her that a long time ago, but she was smart and knew better than me. I just make the trinkets for others to use.

**ANGEL SARAH:** When was the last time you saw Dr. Wren in person?

**VANCE:** She visited my studio months ago to ask about a chain modification for another brooch. Not the one that killed her.

**ANGEL SARAH:** Did she mention any problems she was having?

**VANCE:** Iona was distracted, distant. Her magic felt thinner, tighter, like it was coiled too hard. I didn't pry. She could be snappy, especially if she'd been working with difficult clients.

**ANGEL SARAH:** Did she say anything about the brooch then?

**VANCE:** Not a word. That's why I'm stunned to learn it killed her. It wasn't meant to hurt anyone. It soothed.

**ANGEL SARAH:** You created the brooch found in the victim's possession?

**VANCE:** Yes. Years ago. It wasn't meant to... well, it wasn't meant to do what it did.

**ANGEL SARAH:** Be specific. What was it meant to do?

**VANCE:** Subtle, passive magic. Iona commissioned it as part of her empathic work.

**ANGEL SARAH:** Dr. Wren's work focused on complex client needs. Was the brooch powerful enough to help in such cases?

**VANCE:** Sure. I mean, maybe. I'm not an empath. The brooch was powerful.

**ANGEL SARAH:** More powerful than you registered it to be?

**VANCE:** Um... maybe. I registered it as a Grade two device. Maybe it should have been four or five. I guess I messed up there.

**ANGEL SARAH:** You neglected to register the brooch's true power. Why?

**VANCE:** It was one of my earliest independent commissions. I didn't want it dissected by the registry.

**ANGEL SARAH:** That's a violation of magical artifact regulations.

**VANCE:** I know. But it was good magic. It had power, but only for positive outcomes.

**ANGEL SARAH:** Where were you on the night of Dr. Iona's death?

**VANCE:** In my studio. Alone. I was carving memory bands.

**ANGEL SARAH:** Can anyone confirm that?

**VANCE:** Unless the meaning of the word alone has changed, then, no. But I don't need an alibi. I had no issues with Iona. We respected each other's work.

**ANGEL SARAH:** Have you ever had any other work used in a magical incident such as this?

**VANCE:** Since you're asking, you already know the answer.

**ANGEL SARAH:** For the record, please.

**VANCE:** Once. But a long time ago. A bracelet I made when I was an apprentice was modified. It caused an injury. I was cleared of wrongdoing, but... yes, I carry that shame. Perhaps I could have done more to monitor the bracelet's use. Maybe the magic turned. Maybe someone tampered with it. I can't check every piece of jewelry I make.

**ANGEL SARAH:** Can you think of anyone who would want to harm Dr. Iona?

**VANCE:** Sure. I mean, if you think someone messed with the brooch, then you need to talk to Delphine Noxley. She hated Iona after she got her kicked out of the healers' guild. There was a ton of tension between them. They always bickered. Delphine loved to pick a fight, and she holds grudges.

**ANGEL SARAH:** Thank you. We may have further questions.

**VANCE:** I'll be here. And I'm always happy to help.

**Follow up**

**Artifact analysis**: Conduct a magical forensic sweep of the brooch to identify alterations to its enchantments and compare the current magical signature to the original attunement records (if available) from Crispin Vance's workshop.

**Ritual circle investigation**: Reconstruct the partially drawn ritual circle from the crime scene and cross-reference it with known celestial alignment diagrams, particularly those linked to empathy-channeled alignment work.

**Alibi:** Canvas the nearby stores/residences in Glint Alley for sightings of Vance on the night of Dr. Wren's death.

# Chapter 6

While I waited for the snow globe to settle and reconnect, Minnie snuffled around the desk, disturbing Iona's file notes.

I gently nudged her away. "Stay still. You're distorting the snow globe magic."

Minnie thumped the top of the snow globe. "This is an antique. You could sell it for a fortune."

"I'm never selling it. It's my only way of communicating with home. Now hush, I see Sage appearing."

Sage's glare was fixed on Minnie. "This is a private conversation."

"Minnie's included," I said. "After all, it was her witch who died."

Minnie sniffed loudly. "Now I have Juno helping, we'll soon figure out what happened to Iona."

"Don't be so sure. She's not as smart as she looks," Sage said.

Minnie regarded me solemnly. "Is that true? I'm never sure about white cats. It's all the fur, you see. It gets everywhere. It's like a fluffy smokescreen."

"I like to leave my mark," I said. "And I prefer to think of it as white glitter. It's always welcome."

"It isn't when Vorana gets it in her mouth," Sage said. "Anyway, I read through Crispin's interview with Angel Force. Is there any mention of a follow-up after he was questioned? And did they run a sweep over the hexed heart to see if the enchantments were altered?"

I referenced a page in the case file. "There was a distortion in the magic, but Angel Force couldn't determine whether it was because someone had deliberately altered it or the magic malfunctioned due to age."

"Age is cruel to all of us," Sage said. "Every day I'm limping more."

"You only do that to get sympathy and extra treats from Vorana."

"It works, so I'll keep doing it," Sage said. "What about the magical signature in Crispin's workshop?"

"Nothing useful was found," I said. "Crispin works with enchanted gems and gold every day, so his workshop is full of the stuff. The angels looked, but they found nothing conclusive to tie to the hexed heart."

"Did they recreate the circle they found at the crime scene?" Sage asked.

"A request went in, but it got held up by red tape and never happened. Even decades ago, Angel Force was as lazy as they are now." I turned to Minnie. "Do you remember anything about Iona drawing a circle of protection on the night of her death? Did she need protecting from something?"

Minnie hemmed and hawed for a few seconds. "I wish I could remember, but I don't recall a circle.

Then again, I recall little about that evening. It's all a blur."

"How convenient," Sage muttered.

"Did Angel Force ask around at any of the other stores to see about Crispin's alibi?" Sage asked. "Find out if he'd been seen in his workshop that night?"

"According to a handwritten note, they went door to door," I said, "but no one confirmed Crispin was there. There was a record that lights were left on that evening, but that's all."

"That means nothing," Sage said. "He could have turned on the lights, made the place appear occupied, and then gone out to deal with Iona."

"It means he's still a suspect," I said.

"What about the previous incident, where another piece of his jewelry harmed someone?" Sage asked. "It seems Crispin is a repeat offender of magical mishaps."

"Can you look into that for me?" I asked. "There's no information in this file."

"What a surprise," Sage said. "I'll put it on my list of things to do. What are you planning next?"

"I'm visiting Glint Alley. Crispin still has a workshop there, doesn't he?" I asked Minnie.

"Oh, sure. I can't ever see Crispin leaving Badger's Haze. His family started their business here."

"You know Crispin well?" Sage asked.

"He used to work with Iona, but that was a while ago," Minnie said. "When she was getting going in her career. She soon realized she was far more powerful than him and moved on, leaving Crispin to stare open-mouthed at how incredible my witch was."

"He could have been resentful about that," I said. "That's a motive."

"What's he like?" Sage asked. "Do you think he'll talk about what happened to Iona all those years ago?"

"I can't remember how he acted at the time of her death," Minnie said. "But then, like I said—"

"You don't remember much. Yeah, we get it," Sage groused.

"Crispin sounded surprised during his interview," I said. "He asked lots of questions to find out what happened to Iona."

"Killers can go one of two ways," Sage said. "They either overshare because they think it'll make them look helpful, or they don't talk at all."

"Do you think he's innocent?" I asked Minnie.

She scratched behind one ear. "I'm not sure about him. We should talk to him."

"There's no time like the present. Shall we?"

"You can't take Minnie with you!" Sage said. "She's supposed to be dead. If anyone reports her to Angel Force, they'll arrest her."

"Who would do that?" I asked.

"The villagers keep to themselves because most of them are in trouble with the angels already," Minnie muttered. "Although there are a few around here who stick to the law, so I should be careful."

"Why shouldn't they break the rules when there are no angels left to enforce them?" I asked.

"Badger's Haze has been abandoned," Minnie said forlornly. "I'm sure Angel Force hopes this place will blow up in a magical tornado of mischief."

"Let's hope it doesn't come to that. At least not while I'm living here," I said. "But Sage is right."

"I always am," Sage said. "What am I right about this time?"

"Minnie suddenly showing up will stir the gossip. You need a disguise."

"There's a box of old wigs down in the library basement," Minnie said.

"I'm thinking more of a magical disguise," I said. "What have you got?"

"Oh, I see. My magic is more to do with feelings rather than physical alteration. I can do something with one of those wigs. There was a long blonde one, very soft. I've slept on it once or twice."

"Juno should cast a spell to transform you. It'll test the limits of her new magic and show me exactly how much she's been practicing," Sage said. There was a wicked glint in her eyes. "Go on. Fashion a remodel spell on Minnie."

I wasn't sure I could trust my magic to perform such a delicate spell. But what was the worst that could happen?

"Are you happy for me to disguise you?" I asked Minnie. "You'd still be a cat. You'd just look different."

"I can't look any worse than this, so do what you need to," Minnie said. "And once we're done, I'll show you a back route to Glint Alley. That means fewer people will see us wandering about.

I've heard the gossip about you, so I know you're not popular around here."

"I'm more popular than I used to be," I said. "But that's a good idea. Let me focus so I don't make a mistake and turn you blue."

Sage chuckled and muttered under her breath, no doubt saying something rude about my dubious magic.

I tuned her out and listened to the waves of magic pulsing through me. The magic Eliza Thorny had gifted me for solving her murder was a strange blend of warm and cold. She'd been an expert in fire magic but had developed her skills with water before her death.

Hot and cold sensations trickled through me, reluctant to move, like black treacle sliding out of a bottle.

Magic sparkled on my paws, and I pressed them lightly to Minnie's side. A patch of fur turned bright orange, then striped like a tiger.

"Is that the look you were going for?" Sage asked. "Minnie doesn't exactly blend in, looking like a stunted wildcat."

"Let me try again." I refocused, gently stroking the magic from the tip of Minnie's nose down to her straggly tail. She remained very orange and very tiger-like.

Minnie looked over her new coloring and then roared.

"Do you like it?" I asked.

"I look incredible. Thank you!" Minnie spun around several times, showing off her new look.

"You'll definitely need to stick to the back streets looking like that," Sage said. "Just make sure that magic holds."

Minnie kept roaring and stalking around, swatting at any ghost who got close, so I swiftly signed off with Sage, and we left the library.

Outside, it was a damp, dubious sort of day. The kind of day you'd rather spend hiding under a duvet, binge-eating your favorite treats, and watching reruns of your favorite programs.

"You lead the way," I said to Minnie, checking there was no one around as we headed away from the library.

Minnie strutted with her chin up, looking the epitome of a tiny tiger. "It feels good to be out without watching my back. Even though Angel Force abandoned this place, I'm still sure I'll be arrested any second."

"You've spent all these years on your own?" I asked. "That must have been terribly lonely."

"You get used to it," Minnie said. "And I came to the conclusion that every night would be my last. When I'd wake the next morning, I couldn't decide if I was grateful or miserable to be breathing. There must be something wrong with me to keep going, even though Iona's dead."

"Wrong or incredible? A steely determination for justice is a powerful motivator," I said. "You want to find out what happened to your witch."

"I do! With every fiber of my new, stripy being." Minnie huffed a breath. "But I got lost. My head gave up. I even thought I had gone mad for a few years. Maybe I still am. Do you think I'm mad?"

"You have a charming eccentricity about you," I said.

"Yeah, exactly. That's what I said. Mad as a hatter. This way." Minnie led me along an alleyway that grew steadily less pleasant as we tramped through the damp.

"We go left, right, right, right, left, I think," Minnie said. "That'll get us to Glint Alley. The alley used to be full of independent stores. There's Crispin's place, which is still going. There was a bridal store, a specialist antique place, and also a really fancy cake store. They're all gone now, apart from Crispin. Boarded up since no one has any money to spend on fancy stuff."

"How does Crispin keep going?" I asked.

"He gets outside commissions, I think. That's what he used to do, anyway. And he's a consultant for a few big companies. That's what Iona told me. She said he sold out to the corporations. I don't really understand it. I have no head for business, although I now have the mighty stripes of a warrior." Minnie roared again.

"Maybe less roaring? We're keeping a low profile," I said. "Did you ever think Crispin killed Iona?"

Minnie stumbled over a discarded cardboard box and almost lost her balance. "He was jealous of how powerful she was, but they'd sort of lost touch. She'd use him as a consultant occasionally, but it was more to confirm what she already knew, and also not to tread on his toes."

"Iona was considerate of other people?"

"Um... not always. Don't get me wrong, she was amazing, but sometimes she'd get obsessed over a project, and she hated to fail any client," Minnie said. "Watch out for the rat droppings. Of course, some of her clients were beyond saving. They were too broken, and no matter how much magic she used on them, she had to let them go."

"That sounds emotionally draining," I said.

"Yeah. It was grim. When we had a failure, Iona wouldn't leave her bed for days. I'd snuggle next to her while she recuperated and feed her healing energy."

"What a difficult bond to maintain." I glanced at Minnie, who was inspecting the stripes on one of her legs with a look of deep satisfaction.

"That's what I've always done. It was always us, healing the world. Or at least trying to. Here it is." Minnie stopped outside a faded, tired-looking store with a black door.

I had to stretch up and ring the bell to get entry. A moment later, a tall man with broad shoulders and a thick head of dark hair threaded with gray opened the door.

"I don't believe I have any appointments scheduled for this time," the man said.

"Greetings. I'm Juno, and this is my companion, Stripe," I said. "I hope you don't mind our showing up unannounced."

"I always welcome new clients. I'm Crispin Vance, the owner. What is it you seek? A new collar, perhaps?"

"Yes, I absolutely need a new collar. And it must be full of enchantments," I said.

"Then you've come to the right place. Please come inside. I have pre-made stock available, although it'll need to be adjusted to your precise measurements." Crispin stepped back and let us into the store. It was a small, squat place with a low ceiling, glass cabinets full of jewelry, and muted lighting.

"If I'm not mistaken, you're the cat living in the library. Is that right?" Crispin asked, giving me an appraising look.

"Yes, although it's a temporary situation," I said.

"It's good someone is keeping an eye on the place," Crispin said. "The last librarian fled over three years ago."

"What did she flee from?" I asked.

"Some say the library ghosts, although I've always found them pleasant. At least they were before the place shut," Crispin said. "But there was a rumor that something foul stalked her at night. A trouble spirit attached itself to her and wouldn't let go."

"That wasn't me!" Minnie said. "Even though I look like a tiger, I'm more like a baby kitten."

"Isn't that the very definition of a kitten? A baby cat?" Amusement gleamed in Crispin's eyes.

"Yes, that's what I meant," Minnie said, looking a touch confused.

"Let me show you my collection of collars, and you can try some on." Crispin led us to a glass counter and extracted a tray of collars. "They all have small attachments for pouches, so you can carry charms, potions, whatever you like, really. The design is clever. One of my own."

I loathed collars, and I definitely didn't want to wear one. But actually, having a collar full of different enchantments was a genius idea, and I'd fashioned my own in the past. It could serve as a backup while I got a handle on my new magic and worked to regain some of my own.

"Is there anything here you'd like to try on?" Crispin asked.

"They all look excellent. Your craftsmanship is remarkable." I studied a thin collar with a silver thread running through the crimson.

"Thank you. How did you hear of my work?" Crispin asked.

"I used to know Dr. Iona Wren," I said.

"Goodness! That's a name I haven't heard in a long time." Crispin almost dropped the tray of collars. "How is that possible? Iona has been dead for many years."

"I'm a lot older than I appear," I said. "But I'll never forget her. I remember her recommending your services."

"Well... I'm grateful she recommended me. And surprised," Crispin said.

"You didn't work together?" I asked.

"Not for a long time. Try this one on." Crispin clipped a dark red collar around my neck, and I instantly felt the trickle of enchantments surrounding me.

"But you did know her?"

"Naturally. Our paths crossed in a professional capacity many times," Crispin said. "What do you think of the collar?"

"It's a good fit. Did you enjoy working with Iona?" I asked.

"She was talented."

"She was the best," Minnie said. "At least, so I heard. We never met. I'm always too busy, out stalking prey and roaring at troublemakers, to spend time with powerful witches."

"Her death was a tragedy." I admired myself in a small mirror Crispin propped up. "She died because of a hexed brooch you gave her, isn't that right?"

"Oh, no!" Crispin said. "Well, that's the basics of the story, but there's a lot more to it than that."

I looked up at him, waiting for him to continue.

"Let's try you in something else," Crispin said. "How about this blue one?"

"I like the red," I said. "I'm slightly concerned that if Iona died because of an enchanted piece of jewelry you created, then perhaps your magic isn't stable."

Crispin huffed out a breath. "I produce the finest enchanted pieces of jewelry within five hundred miles. I've even served royalty. My magic is entirely stable."

"So, what happened to Iona?" I asked. "It was the hexed heart, wasn't it?"

"That piece of jewelry was more symbolic," Crispin said. "And I've always despised that nickname. I never filled it with powerful magic. If someone tampered with it—and I'm not saying it was Iona—then that was out of my control."

"Do you ever get asked to create jewelry that's excessively powerful?" I asked. "Pieces that could harm others?"

"If I'm ever asked such an absurd thing, I always refuse," Crispin said. "I have a reputation to maintain."

"And it's a fine reputation," I said. "Your craftsmanship would be a joy to wear."

"Hmmm... perhaps this isn't for you." Crispin unclipped the red collar.

"Oh no, I absolutely want a collar," I said quickly. "Although I'm short on funds. Perhaps we could do a trade."

Crispin's gaze narrowed as he stared at Minnie. "Why has your tail changed color?"

Minnie whirled around. "How strange. It's never done that before. Maybe I'm sick. What illness changes fur color?"

Crispin slid the collars back into the glass case and locked it. "It's time you both left."

"I really want a collar," I said. "Is there nothing I could do to convince you to give me one?"

"You could pay me, just like everyone else does," Crispin said curtly.

"Did Iona ever buy enchanted jewelry from you?" I asked.

"That's quite enough," Crispin snapped. "I understand some individuals have a morbid fascination with the macabre, but it's not a suitable topic of conversation. Iona was a respected member of this community, and there's no point in stirring up what happened to her. After all this time, it's deeply disrespectful. I must ask you both to leave." He strode to the door, yanked it open, and barked, "And don't come back."

I glanced at Minnie and noticed her orange fur was shifting in patches, the stripes fading to blotches of muddy brown. The disguise was failing!

We bolted out of the store, and the door slammed shut behind us.

"Your magic is misbehaving," Minnie said, eyeing her tail as the stripes bled into blotches. "Can't I keep my tiger stripes forever? I love them. They make me feel so powerful."

"I wish I could grant that request," I said. "But I'm still learning how to use magic again."

"Oh! I thought it felt like strange magic," Minnie gave her chest fur a half-hearted lick. "Don't worry. I like being black and white. It suits me."

I glanced back. Crispin glared at us through the window. His face was all sharp edges and suspicion. "What did you make of him? He didn't want to discuss Iona. Do you think he's guilty?"

"Like I said, he was jealous of how amazing she was," Minnie said.

"Is that enough of a motive to kill?"

We turned down a damp street, our paws splashing through an unavoidable puddle.

"I don't remember Crispin being around much after Iona dropped him," Minnie said.

"That actually gives him a better motive," I said. "Crispin wanted to keep working with Iona, but she outgrew him. Maybe he confronted her, they argued, and she belittled him. Are you sure you can't remember if he was there the night Iona died?"

"I mean... he could have been there," Minnie said, her voice low. "And he would know how to tamper with the brooch. Enough to make it misfire."

"Enough to kill Iona," I said. "He has the skills. And since he claimed he was working late on his own the night Iona died, he stays on the suspect list."

Minnie let out one last roar before the orange dissolved completely. In a blink, she was back to her usual adorable scruffy black-and-white self.

"What do we do now?" she asked.

"We keep poking at suspects," I said, "until one cracks and tells us what they really did to your wonderful witch."

# Chapter 7

"And that was when my tail changed color and Crispin threw us out of his store!" Minnie spun in a circle, as if to show her colors, even though she was back to being a black cat with splodges of white and cute white socks.

"That magic you were gifted isn't as reliable as I hoped it would be," Sage muttered to me, glancing over her shoulder for what seemed like the dozenth time.

We were back in the library after being tossed out of Crispin's store. I'd updated Sage on our discovery and that Crispin needed to remain a suspect in Iona's murder.

She'd whispered to me that Minnie should stay on the list too, but I pretended not to hear. Of course, Minnie had to remain a suspect, but I enjoyed having the company. Even if that company might have ended her witch's life.

Being banished to a fading magical village full of corruption and suspicion was a lonely business, and I worked better when I had friends around me. Crime solving was easier that way. Or at least more entertaining.

But I wasn't naïve. I still watched Minnie. So far, aside from some eccentricities, such as howling at odd hours, pacing in repeated circles, and her constant clumsiness, which I suspected had more to do with her singular vision than anything else, I'd discovered nothing that made me suspicious of her.

Minnie's stomach growled loudly, and mine soon joined in.

"We need more tinned ham!" Minnie said.

"You ate the last tin," I replied.

"I know places where we can scavenge for food. It might be moldy, but it's still edible."

"Mold is never edible," Sage said. "Not even on cheese. I don't know how people enjoy that disgusting, stinky stuff they insist is delicious. It smells like scabby feet and stomach bile."

"You get used to it," Minnie said. "I can take us there now."

"You're not going anywhere." Sage looked over her shoulder again.

"What are you up to?" I asked. "You've been distracted ever since we came back."

"Just wait. It's a surprise," Sage said. "I've been working on something."

"Have you finally gotten the angels to see sense and reprieve me?" I asked with a hint of hope in my voice.

"There's more chance of hell freezing over, turning into an eternal ice rink, and then Angel Force hosting the Olympics," Sage said.

"So, what is it then?" I asked.

"Come on, I'm starving!" Minnie said. "There's barely moldy food for us to gobble down. I know all the best spots. A lot of houses have been abandoned, but people never cleared their cupboards. There'll be a feast waiting for us."

"A moldy, gross feast," Sage muttered. "Stay where you are. She's coming."

My heart skipped a beat. Sage had turned around, so I could only see the back of her harness, her legs strapped in tight.

"Sage, what's going on?" I asked.

Sage turned back, an excited gleam in her eyes. "Zandra's here!"

I leaned so close to the snow globe that I bumped it with my booping snooter. "I don't see her. Get her to come nearer."

"She's right behind me," Sage said. "Lean down so Juno can see you properly. Finn convinced Cythera to let her out for good behavior."

I squinted, but I still couldn't see her.

Sage chuckled and glanced up.

"What did Zandra say?" I stamped my paw. "There's something wrong with the snow globe."

"Hold on. This happened before when we tried to connect you," Sage said. "Thump it. I'll do the same on my end."

This wasn't the first time I'd tried to speak with Zandra through the globe network. The last few times, my globe had fizzled out and died. So, this was progress. Of sorts.

I jiggled the globe, pressed a few random knobs on the side, and stared at the glittering flakes drifting around. Sage had vanished from view.

"Can you see Zandra now? She's right in front of the globe," Sage said.

My breath fogged the glass as I pressed closer, my pulse pitter-pattering, willing the image to appear so I could glimpse the most incredible witch ever to walk this planet.

"Were you banished here?" Minnie asked.

"Yes. Incorrectly so," I said. "What does that matter?"

"It was Angel Force that punished you?"

"Technically, the higher angels. The eccentric ones. They float around, passing obscure laws and generally making a nuisance of themselves."

"That's why you can't see your witch," Minnie said.

"What do you mean?" I asked.

"If you were sent here as punishment, the higher angels would've taken away all your privileges. That includes spending time with the witch you're bonded to. They know that would be your greatest wish, so they make sure you can't do it. It's part of your sentence."

I planted both front paws firmly on the snow globe and growled. "Every time we've tried to connect, there's been a malfunction."

"Uh oh. That means the angels are watching what we're doing," Sage said.

"They can see I'm helping them! Does that mean nothing to them?"

"Hold on a second," Sage said. "Zandra's cursing so loudly I can barely hear you."

"Try to stay calm," I said, even though Zandra wouldn't be able to hear me.

"I'm trying!" Sage said. "But she's blasting out magic now."

"I meant Zandra. Oh, never mind." I looked up at the ceiling. I don't know why. The only things up there were spiders, dust, and cobwebs, but it felt appropriate to look skyward when talking to angels. "If you're monitoring my every move, then you can see I'm doing good. You sent me here to make amends. I've already solved one of your cases. I'm not a bad magic user, I just made a few tiny mistakes. Everyone deserves a second chance."

"You've had more than a few chances," Sage muttered. She raised a paw when I glared at her. "I mean, you've never exactly treated Angel Force with respect."

"Have they done anything to earn my respect?" I snarled. Magic sparked across my fur, heating me from the inside out.

"Wow! How did you do that?" Sage asked.

Magic vibrated through me, then burst out, swirling around in a glittering mist.

"Maybe my borrowed magic operates under rage conditions. That could be the answer," I said. "If I fuel myself with fury at the injustice served to me, I'll become more powerful."

"That's a terrible idea," Sage said. "Rage magic never ends well."

"I wouldn't do that," Minnie added. "Living a life full of rage would be miserable."

"It'll end well for me if I can get back to Crimson Cove." I channeled my fury, thinking about how unfairly I'd been treated, stuck in this magical backwater. Friendless. Witchless. Always hungry. Sleeping on piles of moldy paper. Harassed by library rats. Haunted by Shakespeare-quoting ghosts.

The magic that had blasted out of me fizzled away.

"Huh. Maybe rage has nothing to do with it, and that was a magical hiccup," I said, defeat whacking me aside the head and making me slump.

"Zandra's asking if you're feeling okay," Sage said.

"Of course I'm not! I miss her. Tell her that. Make sure she knows I'll be home soon."

"Is that a promise you can keep?" Sage asked.

"I will keep it, no matter what I have to do to get home." A sticky wave of disappointment slid over me, and I flopped onto the desk. "You were both right. Rage isn't the answer to anything."

"Then what is?" Minnie asked.

"Solving the unsolvable case," I replied. "We focus on finding out what happened to Iona. It's time to look at our next suspect. Sage, here's Delphine Noxley's interview."

**Case File:** #2001-1020
**Subject:** Noxley, Delphine
**Interviewer:** Angel Sarah
**Location:** Angel Force Field Office, Badger's Haze

**ANGEL SARAH:** Please state your full name and magical occupation for the record.
**NOXLEY:** Delphine Noxley. Healer. Former healer, technically. I suppose that makes me unofficially retired.

Imagine that. At my age.

**ANGEL SARAH:** What was your relationship to Dr. Iona Wren?

**NOXLEY:** Relationship? Ha. If you can call snapping at each other during guild meetings a relationship, then sure, we had one. We argued all the time. Oil and water. Some people rub you the wrong way, and Iona rubbed against me like a cheese grater on bare skin.

**ANGEL SARAH:** You'd describe your relationship as hostile?

**NOXLEY:** How astute of you. This was mutual dislike. We didn't throw potions at each other, but yes, we were enemies. I never pretended otherwise. Everyone knew about it, so why lie to you?

**ANGEL SARAH:** Did you ever threaten her?

**NOXLEY:** Not in so many words. But I didn't hide my distrust of her. She knew where she stood with me, and I knew she was a fake.

**ANGEL SARAH:** What did she fake?

**NOXLEY:** It would be easier to give you a list of her genuine acts. She did everything she could to make my life hard. She's the reason I can't practice anymore. The high and mighty Dr. Iona Wren greased the right palms and had my license revoked.

**ANGEL SARAH:** Why would she do

that?

**NOXLEY:** I was a threat to her business. She said I was taking her clients because I charged less. She was way too expensive, but hated to admit it, so she came after me.

**ANGEL SARAH:** And how do you feel about her death?

**NOXLEY:** Relieved. Is that what you want to hear? I'm not weeping into my tea. Now, I can work on getting my license back and practice again without her bleating about me making her look bad. She made herself look bad by having twice the hourly rate I do. You know what that's called? Greed. It's no wonder she's dead.

**ANGEL SARAH:** You understand statements like that could be interpreted as a motive for wanting her dead?

**NOXLEY:** You'll interpret it however it suits your report. I won't pretend I liked her. But that doesn't mean I killed her.

**ANGEL SARAH:** Where were you on the night of Dr. Wren's death?

**NOXLEY:** Sleeping. Alone. I recently broke up with a guy. He was a jerk, but I was having some me time before diving back into the murky, shark-infested dating waters. You get bit a few times, and it makes you wary. You know what I mean?

**ANGEL SARAH:** No one can verify that?

**NOXLEY:** That I was taking a break from dating losers?

**ANGEL SARAH:** That you were home alone?

**NOXLEY:** Nope.

**ANGEL SARAH:** Can you think of anyone else who might have wanted to harm Dr. Wren?

**NOXLEY:** Aside from myself? Probably half the people she overcharged for her inflated sense of self-importance. And you'll want to speak to that weird cat she had as a familiar. Quirky little thing, but creepy too. Always staring with that freaky eye.

**ANGEL SARAH:** Minnie is blind in one eye. Blindness isn't freaky.

**NOXLEY:** If Iona were a proper healer, she'd have fixed that eye.

**ANGEL SARAH:** Are you suggesting she mistreated her familiar?

**NOXLEY:** Why not? She mistreated me. There were men, too. Several. Charming on the surface, but slippery underneath.

**ANGEL SARAH:** Was Dr. Wren dating anyone in particular?

**NOXLEY:** If they were wealthy, handsome, or she just wanted to ruin things for someone else, she'd date them. Iona wasn't fussy about who she got to buy her dinner. Some might say she had issues with her morals and keeping her undies in place.

**ANGEL SARAH:** Is there anything else you'd like to add?

**NOXLEY:** Yes. Stop trying to pin this murder on me. I'm honest enough to admit I wanted her gone, but that doesn't mean I dirtied my hands to do it. I'm glad she's dead, so I never have to think about her again.

## Follow up

The witness displays a confrontational tone and offers no verifiable alibi. She admitted openly to a strong dislike of the victim. However, she denies involvement.

1. Confirm Miss Noxley's whereabouts on the night of the murder by speaking to neighbors
2. Investigate Dr. Wren's known romantic relationships for additional suspects
3. Delphine Noxley is still a suspect

# Chapter 8

The snow globe refused to fire up after I'd sent through Delphine's snappy and far too sharp interview with the no doubt sweet and well-meaning Angel Sarah.

Rather than waiting around to see if the malfunctioning magical tech behaved, I knew action was needed.

"Minnie, do you know where Delphine lives?" I asked.

She was batting a ball of rolled-up paper between her paws. "Delphine had a place on the far side of the village, but when she lost her license to practice, she had to give it up. She spent some time in lodgings, then she went wild."

"What does that mean?"

"She lived in the woods and had an old shack out there. It sounded almost cozy. An outdoor fire, a stream nearby where she could wash, and she was into wild swimming, no matter how cold it was."

I grimaced. "You'll never get me wild swimming. Or any kind of swimming. Tame, semi-tame, or anything in between. Do you know what lives in rivers and seas?"

"Fish," Minnie said. "You're not worried about alligators, are you? Or those fish with the sharp teeth? Pterodactyls, is it?"

"Pterodactyls fly. And they were dinosaurs," I said. "You mean piranhas."

"Yes, those. And some snakes swim in water, too. I chased one once. They bite." Minnie meowed pitifully. "Won't do that again."

"Exactly. Aside from your horrific suggestions, not only are there things in the water that drag you under and eat you, but where do you think fish and sea mammals go to the toilet?" I shuddered. "And where do they, you know, have their sexy times?"

Minnie's eyes widened. "In the water!"

I nodded. "So basically, when you're wild swimming or tame swimming or doing any kind of swimming, you're splashing around in fish effluent and sexy-time fluids. It's unhygienic."

"But if you're swimming in the sea, that's a lot of water to dilute the fluids," Minnie said.

"It's still there. And it will still be matted in your fur weeks later," I said. "Please don't tell me we have to go anywhere near a stream to speak to Delphine."

"Oh no," Minnie said quickly. "Delphine got a bit... weird. She moved into a facility. Or rather, a doctor signed her into a place."

"In Badger's Haze?" I asked.

"Sure. It happened to a few of the older witches who didn't get out in time."

"Before the village had its problems?"

"Yep. The hexing, slithering grossness that descended on this place made magic users lose their way when it was downgraded to a cursed hovel nobody wanted to live in. People wanted to leave but couldn't, so they went strange. Delphine was one of them."

"Are you talking about a secure unit for wayward magic users?" I asked.

"More of a retirement village with bars on the windows and guards." Minnie batted the paper ball again, and a library ghost swooped after it, bumping into a shelf with a crash. "That was the last place I heard Delphine was living. She's been there for a while. She may not even be alive, though."

"Then that's where we'll go to find out."

Minnie flattened her ears. "Do we have to? Delphine is scary. Even when she had her license to practise healing magic, she was terrifying. That's why Iona reported her to the guild. Delphine scared her clients instead of healing them."

"Then she's definitely worth speaking to," I said. "You lead the way."

"If we must. Back roads again?" Minnie asked.

"Since one out of every two villagers currently hates me, that's a good idea."

We took the back way out of the library and wound through a series of ever more depressing alleyways.

"Describe Delphine to me," I said. "Was she as powerful as Iona?"

"Delphine has power," Minnie said. "But it comes with a sharp tang. It wasn't suitable for more vulnerable clients. Especially those dealing with grief or darker emotions."

"It sounds like she was blunt in her delivery." I hopped over a flattened cardboard box that squelched when my paw landed close to it.

"Delphine said she only ever spoke the truth."

"Which was why she was so open when interviewed by that angel," I said.

"They were always arguing," Minnie went on. "Delphine used to barge into Iona's office when she was mid-empathic session. It would ruin everything, and Iona had to start again. She hated that."

"Didn't you guard the door to stop her?" I asked.

"It didn't always work. Delphine could be... determined."

"Iona's only issue with Delphine was her bluntness?"

"That and the fees," Minnie said. "Iona was the best, so she charged a fair rate for her services. Delphine was competent, but not in the same league. She charged half Iona's rate when she set up. Some people couldn't afford Iona, so they turned to Delphine instead. Iona noticed she was losing clients and confronted her about it."

"I imagine Delphine told her where to go."

"Several times. And very loudly." Minnie stopped, her ears swiveling. She checked the street and then flicked her tail. "We need to do the last bit on the main road. We could get noticed."

"We'll hurry. Keep your head down, and try not to bump into anything," I said.

We moved quickly, all conversation stopped. Minnie tripped over her own front paws more than once, but we managed not to draw any attention.

Finally, we stopped outside a rusted side gate. A battered sign read: Fallen Stars Retirement Home.

From a distance, the building behind the gate looked like a stately home with sprawling grounds, but a closer inspection revealed guards patrolling in pairs, and every window had bars.

"They really don't want people getting out," I muttered.

"They're safer inside," Minnie said. "I don't think anyone transfers in these days. It's just the old residents still in there, waiting to die."

"Do they get treatment?" I asked.

"Not anymore," Minnie said. "They used to. It was more proactive when Badger's Haze had a future. But now that there's no outside support, they've been abandoned. Same as the rest of us." She let out a soft howl.

Which meant there was no way to know how bad things had gotten behind those bars. It could be magical carnage or a bunch of elderly, broken witches with nothing to do but puzzles and daydreaming.

I braced myself and tested my magic. It didn't instantly reject me, which I took as a good sign.

"We'll have to sneak in," Minnie whispered. "We won't be on the guest list. If you're not an approved visitor, you don't get past the receptionist."

"We should be able to squeeze through the window bars," I said. "We just need to find an open window."

It took a few minutes of dodging guards and crouching behind hedges, but we finally spotted a lower-floor window left ajar. We slipped through easily, and I was grateful for my slimmer figure. The starvation diet courtesy of Badger's Haze had shaved down my pooch belly.

Inside, the air was stale, with a faint tang of disinfectant. The corridor stretched ahead, lined with closed doors.

"How many people live here?" I whispered.

"Two floors. Forty or fifty residents, maybe," Minnie said.

"We don't want to linger," I said. "Do you know which room Delphine is in?"

"I'll find her," Minnie promised. She lifted her nose, sniffing like a professional tracker. "Delphine smells a bit like Iona. Cotton candy with a lemon tang. It's the healing smell."

We crept down the hall. From behind the closed doors came coughs, mutters, and an occasional burst of laughter. Only a handful of attendants moved about. We ducked out of sight twice, then pressed on.

Minnie halted in front of a door. The label read: Delphine Noxley.

"Well done," I whispered.

Minnie puffed out her chest. "I smell better because I only see out of one eye. Other senses get stronger, you see? Or rather, I don't see as well as you, but I smell better. I mean—"

"I understand. Does Delphine have a familiar?" I asked.

Minnie shook her head. "A few tried to bond with her, but she's spiky, so couldn't find a match."

"Some witches don't bond," I said. "I always find that peculiar. She'd be happier bonded to a familiar.

I know I'm happier now that I have Zandra. I never realized true happiness until I met my witch."

"Same with me and Iona." Minnie's voice dipped.

I pressed the door open. No knocking, no warning. Inside, the curtains were drawn, and the room was cloaked in gloom. A woman lay on the bed. Thin. Motionless.

"She's not dead, is she?" Minnie whispered.

"Only on the inside," the woman rasped.

I tensed, ready for Delphine to spring at us. Instead, she stayed where she was, her head slowly turning toward us.

"Come closer. I only bite when I'm particularly grumpy."

I glanced at Minnie and shrugged. "Greetings. I'm Juno, and this is Minnie."

Delphine's lips curled into something halfway between a smile and a sneer. "Minnie! You're alive. What brings you here?"

"I'm ready to find the truth about Iona's murder," Minnie said, a faint tremor in her voice.

"What are you doing with that reprobate?" Delphine's gaze cut toward me. "You know that's the cursed cat the angels dumped here?"

"Not cursed. And wrongly dumped," I said. "How do you know about my situation?"

"Because there's nothing to do in here except listen to the guards' gossip," Delphine said. "I've heard all about you. You got your nose stuck into some cold case, didn't you? Stopped a sacrifice or some such nonsense."

"That's my purpose," I said. "It's why I'm here. To right wrongs. And it's why we're here to talk to you about Dr. Iona Wren, and about what really happened to her."

Delphine tilted her head. Her eyes glittered with interest, though her mouth kept its sneer. "And how am I supposed to remember something from that long ago?"

"It was a significant event in the village," I said.

"Not for me. Did you bring me anything? Patients should always get gifts."

Minnie winced. "We forgot."

"That's rude. Visitors usually bring food. Or pointless flowers. I hate cut flowers. Give me a cactus in a pot, and at least I'll have a go at keeping it alive. But if you thrust a bouquet at me, you're basically handing me something already dying. That's disturbing. Cut flowers are an awful gift."

"There's a logic to that," I admitted. "My witch doesn't like cut flowers either."

"Like I care. You're wasting your time here. You can leave if you haven't brought me anything." Delphine turned her head away.

"I could check the kitchen," Minnie offered. "They might have cake."

"No, that's all slop." Delphine said with a theatrical sigh.

"You seem bored," I said. "We could keep you company. Wouldn't that be nice?"

"That's one word for it," Delphine muttered.

"Aren't you curious about what I've already found out about Iona's death?" I asked.

"Not particularly. I didn't like her when she was alive, and I still don't like her now she's dead. What do you expect to find after all this time?"

"The truth," I said. "Iona was murdered. Angel Force never figured out who did it. They questioned you, didn't they?"

Delphine's eyes snapped back to mine. For a heartbeat, the sneer dropped, replaced by something darker. "You think it was me?"

Minnie squeaked and backed away.

"In your interview, you were open about hating Iona," I said.

"Sure. And I still do."

"Even after all this time?"

"I'd have killed her myself if someone hadn't done it for me. We were always arguing. Iona got greedy."

"She wasn't greedy! She charged a fair price for her talents," Minnie said.

"She was greedy," Delphine shot back. "You'll always defend her."

Minnie lifted her chin. "That's because Iona was perfect."

"No one is perfect." Delphine finally sat up and adjusted her pillows. "She liked to believe she was, and that's why I disliked her so much. Besides, some people you just don't get along with. You don't know why, but it's as if magic creates friction. My abilities knew there was something off with Iona, and so I reacted against her."

"I can understand you being angry with Iona," I said. "You lost your livelihood because of her."

"It wasn't such a loss. I didn't enjoy working with people," Delphine admitted. "I did my best because that was the magic I inherited, but I was happier in my own company. It's easier that way. Then I only have myself to annoy."

"You didn't mind that you lost the only way you had of making money?" I asked.

"Having money is great, but I've always liked a simple life. I had a dream about owning my own camper, living independently, off-grid. I kept pushing it back, telling myself I'd do it next year, and then the next. It never happened. I got comfortable."

"You lived in the woods, though," I said. "That wasn't simple enough?"

"It was fine. I reduced my hours, so I didn't have to deal with too many people and still made ends meet. But then Iona reported me and told them I was incompetent." Delphine picked at her bitten fingernails. "Apparently, a few clients had complained. With those complaints and Iona's concerns, it didn't take the guild long to revoke my license. They said I could sit the exams after two years to ensure I was competent. I never bothered."

A tap on the door had me diving under the bed, dragging Minnie with me.

"Delphine, are you going out again today?" a female voice called.

"Get lost," she yelled. "I never leave this room, and you know that."

"You're so funny! It's supposed to rain later, so take an umbrella and a groundsheet. Or you can join us for a game of whack-a-mole."

"Go boil your head, Louisa."

The woman chuckled before her footsteps tapped away.

I wriggled out from under the bed. "You can leave here?"

Delphine looked away. "Of course not! Ignore Louisa. She lives in a spooky fantasy world. Her idea of whack-a-mole is chasing other residents with a wooden mallet and trying to bludgeon their brains out."

"You were saying about your old home?" I glanced at the door to ensure Louisa wasn't sneaking in with her mallet to involve us in her game.

"No, I wasn't."

"Why did you leave your place in the woods?" I pressed.

Delphine turned her gaze to the window. "Something... something happened to me in the woods."

"Were you bitten by a water snake?" Minnie asked.

Confusion flickered across Delphine's face. "No, no snakes were involved."

"Then what happened?" I asked.

"I was doing some work for free with a few low-level demons. And before you judge, not all demons are bad. Some reform. Anyway, one demon took offense when I spoke his truth, and let's just say things got messy. I haven't been the same since."

Minnie tapped the floor with a paw. "Wasn't there an incident where you blew something up? And tried to hex a few angels?"

"Maybe. I forget," Delphine said. "Anyway, after the whole demon issue, the explosions, and the angel hexing, it was decided this was the best place for me."

"That sounds intense," I said. "And unfair. Did you have a chance to plead your case? Or get help with your demon issue?"

"No. And I deserved it. I was dealing with the wrong crowd, and you know what happens when you get involved with crooked types."

I nodded. "There are usually two routes. One, you get away with it and become rich and famous. Or two, you get trampled, squashed into the dirt, and dumped in a place like this for the rest of your life."

Delphine snorted. "Yeah. And you can see which way I went."

"Did you direct any of your magical issues toward Iona?" I asked.

"I didn't kill Iona." Delphine's voice had lowered. "I might have, but someone got there first. The way I was back then, I'd have probably messed it up, anyway."

"You could get help," I said. "Get your magic stable. Find a purpose. Get out of here."

"No one helps the people who live in Badger's Haze," Delphine replied. "I'm fine with how my life turned out. Sure, it's hardly a laugh a minute, but this place is secure, and they don't let any demons in. They normally don't let annoying cats in to bother you during nap time either. It's all good."

"Can you think of anyone who wanted Iona dead?" I asked. "You mentioned in your interview with Angel Force that she was involved with a few different men. Anyone in particular stand out?"

"Oh, sure. She loved the guys. Iona was a full-on flirt. She had so many guys in her life that I got exhausted just watching her churn through them."

"That's untrue," Minnie snapped. "Iona was looking for the right man. She was even engaged!"

"Like that would have lasted if she'd lived." Delphine smirked.

I turned toward the door as footsteps approached. "Quick! Hide." I shoved Minnie under the bed just as the door opened.

"It's time for your medication, Delphine," a sing-song female voice announced as footsteps crossed the room.

"Oh, joy. I was just getting my senses back and wondering about breaking out of here," Delphine muttered. "What cocktail of delights have you got for me today?"

"The usual. Health and happiness in a few tiny pills. Here you go." A pill pot rattled. "Good girl."

"Aren't I? You can pat my head if you like." Delphine's tone dripped with sarcasm. "Now, get lost."

"It's always a delight to see you. I'll be back in a few hours for your top-up," the nurse replied before leaving and shutting the door.

"You two need to go," Delphine said. "These drugs knock me out for hours."

I scrambled out from under the bed, shaking a few dust bunnies from my fur. "Are you really sure you're happy here? It doesn't seem much fun."

"It's enough for me." Delphine had already closed her eyes, her hands folded over her stomach. "And the meds are out of this world. Now get lost before I raise the alarm and you two end up in here as well."

After checking the corridor, we darted out the same window we'd used to get in. I landed lightly and waited for Minnie to scramble through. She tumbled out, landed on her side, then sprang up and shook her fur.

"What did you make of that?" I asked as we hurried away, making sure none of the guard patrols noticed us.

"Although Delphine wasn't as powerful as Iona, she was strong enough to mess with a piece of jewelry with emotional resonance," Minnie said. "And I'd seen her lurking around Iona's house."

"Lurking? Why did she do that?"

"I figured she was spying on Iona to learn who her clients were and poach them," Minnie said. "But maybe she was figuring out a way to break in and use the hexed heart against Iona."

"Delphine has more than one motive," I said. "Jealousy of Iona's success. Bitterness over losing her career because of Iona."

"And Delphine has no alibi," Minnie added.

I stopped at the gates and turned back to the looming building. "Where do you think she goes?"

"What do you mean?" Minnie's ears twitched.

"The other patient who knocked on the door said Delphine would need an umbrella because rain was due today. Are patients allowed to leave?"

"I don't think so," Minnie said. "Otherwise, there wouldn't be bars on the windows and this massive gate for us to squeeze through."

"We should wait here a while," I said. "See exactly where Delphine sneaks off to."

# Chapter 9

We took turns loitering outside the boundary of the secure unit, shuffling off now and again for comfort breaks or, in Minnie's case, vanishing and returning with snacks she'd found.

Damp air clung to everything, seeping into my fur until it puffed up like a startled hedgehog. We'd wedged ourselves under a lump of dripping foliage, trying to stay dry while also invisible. It partly worked.

"Maybe she's not coming out," Minnie muttered, crunching something stale.

"The way Delphine snapped at that other patient told me otherwise," I said. "She didn't want anyone to know about her secret trips."

"They're not secret if other people know what she's up to," Minnie said, licking crumbs off her whiskers. "Let's go back to the library. My paws are freezing. Maybe we can find another tin of ham to share."

"Another thirty minutes," I said. "If Delphine sneaks out, it'll be after dark. Fewer staff. Fewer witnesses."

Minnie gave a dramatic shiver. "If I were sneaking anywhere, I'd do it at night, too. It's easier to get away with murder that way."

I glanced at her. "How would you know?"

She shrugged. "Just saying. It makes sense. I'm a sensible sort of cat. Do you want to try a pork rind? They're only a year out of date."

I declined and kept watching.

We were about to give up when a shadow darted along the lawn. A small, hunched figure. Then, it was gone.

"Was that Delphine?" I was suddenly on the alert.

"It was the right size," Minnie said, squinting. "What shall we do?"

We scrambled out, shook off damp leaves, and hurried after her. For a moment, I lost sight of the shadow, but there it was, slipping through the far side of the fence.

"It's her!" I hissed. "She knows a secret way out."

"It's probably a hidden gate or door," Minnie said. "It wouldn't take more than a simple unlock spell to get it open, and that's child's play for someone like Delphine."

We stayed well back, keeping to the gloom, mimicking Delphine's secretive shuffle to minimize being noticed. She glanced over her shoulder every few steps, her head down, shoulders hunched, moving like someone carrying a guilty conscience in her pockets.

"She's heading for the edge of the village," Minnie whispered. "There's nothing out there except trees."

"And the cemetery," I said. "Do you think she's visiting someone?"

"Possibly. But why sneak out if it's innocent?"

"Because she's considered dangerous," I muttered. "There's no way the staff would let her wander off alone."

"Surely if she wanted to pay respects, they'd allow it with supervision. It would be cruel to prevent her from grieving and paying her respects to the dead."

We kept following, and after fifteen minutes, she proved my theory right, and Delphine veered toward the cemetery gates.

"Is she friendly with Morticia and Midnight?" I asked. "They don't appreciate uninvited guests. Trust me, I've experienced that unpleasant welcome."

"Morticia isn't friendly with anyone," Minnie said. "Apart from the corpses, although some of them only behave because they fear her."

"If Delphine gets caught trespassing, she's finished."

"Unless she's got an arrangement with Morticia," Minnie murmured. "Maybe she pays her to look the other way. Morticia has a stone for a heart, but she understands grief and loss. After all, she's surrounded by it. She breathes it in."

We slowed, watching as Morticia stopped by the high iron fence. She placed both hands on separate bars and then pulled. A flare of magic sparked from between her palms, and she kept pulling until there was a gap large enough for her to squeeze through.

"She definitely doesn't have an invitation," I said.

"Neither do we," Minnie said. "We should turn back. It's never wise to go inside the cemetery when you're not expected."

I swallowed my concern. "We have no choice. We'll have to take the risk."

Minnie hesitated, then nodded. "I'll do it for Iona. If this helps us get to the truth, whatever it takes."

We raced to the gap Delphine had made with her magic. It was just closing, but we leaped through. I wasn't sure how we'd get out, but that was a problem for another time.

Crouching low to the ground, I took a few seconds to get my bearings and see where Delphine was headed.

"She's heading west," Minnie whispered, pointing with her nose.

"Which part of the cemetery is that?" I asked.

"I think it's full over there, so it'll be older burials," Minnie said. "The new graves are on the other side."

"Delphine could be visiting a relative," I said. "Perhaps it's an important anniversary."

We shuffled along, staying close to the ground. It was times like this when I wished my fur wasn't quite so splendidly white. It stuck out in such gloomy conditions.

"She's stopped!" Minnie said. "And she's looking down at a grave. Now she's speaking."

We crept closer, concealing ourselves behind a high rectangular mausoleum with a stone witch lying in state, her hands across her chest, a stone wand clasped in one hand.

I peeked around the side. We were close enough to hear Delphine.

"Maybe I should ask them to look into what happened to you," she muttered, one hand resting on the headstone.

I was too far away to read the stone's inscription, but it was clear Delphine was familiar with whoever rested beneath her feet.

"She didn't deserve you. I always knew she was wrong and had a rotten heart. Especially after what she did to you."

"Who is she talking about?" I whispered to Minnie.

Minnie shook her head. "Delphine never had many friends. She has a sharp tongue and is never afraid to speak her mind, even if that offends. It doesn't make her popular, so it could be anyone she crossed wands with."

We settled in and watched as Delphine continued to talk to the headstone.

"I don't know how they'll find out anything new. Not after all this time," she said. "It's too late."

"Is she talking about us?" I asked.

"That can't be right. Iona was kind. Delphine said something about a rotten heart. My witch was the opposite of rotten."

"Delphine doesn't think so," I replied. "And I can see why, since she lost her career because of Iona."

"Iona only reported her because she was worried about the clients," Minnie said. "Iona always had people's best interests at heart."

"Delphine wouldn't have thought so," I whispered.

Delphine paused and rifled through the oversized purse hanging over her shoulder. She kept looking inside before crouching and dumping the contents on the ground. She searched through it all, putting each item back one at a time before tipping back her head and letting out a loud sigh.

"I forgot to bring it. I'll have to go back." She gathered the rest of her items, slung the purse over her shoulder, and headed off.

I nudged Minnie into action, and we dashed to the headstone.

The inscription read: *Here lies Vanhoff Randolph. Beloved son and brother. Taken too soon.* The date of his death was January 2001.

"He died the same year as Iona," I said.

"I know that name!" Minnie tilted her head from side to side as she reread the inscription. "I think Iona dated him."

"Was it serious?" I asked.

"They were together a few months, but then Iona got a big new client and had to set aside everything else apart from her work. She was like that. Sometimes it consumed her, and she forgot about everything else." Minnie glanced at me.

"Including you?"

"She could be forgetful, but I know she never meant it," Minnie said. "And we always had our bond. If ever I worried about losing her, I'd tug on that and make sure we were still together."

"That sounds lonely," I said.

"We make sacrifices for the ones we love," Minnie replied.

I looked back at the grave. "Iona and Vanhoff dated, then they split up, and he died. How did you not know Vanhoff was dead?"

"Why would I?" Minnie asked. "Iona was never serious about anybody. She lost contact with all her former boyfriends. Why keep in touch when they were no longer dating?"

"Vanhoff died in January, and Iona was dead less than a year later. Is that a coincidence or is there a connection here?" I asked.

A swirl of icy air whisked around the headstone, ruffling my fur and chilling my toe beans. The sky was too black, with ominous dark clouds and a crackle of lightning overhead. "That's not a natural storm."

Minnie hissed softly. "Oh, rats! It's Morticia. She must know we're here. And she's not happy about it."

The ground trembled. A few seconds later, a pair of gleaming yellow eyes appeared in the shadows.

"Oh, it's just Midnight," I said. "We'll be fine."

Minnie was already backing away. "Morticia controls Midnight, and if she's not happy with us being here, then he'll chase us away."

I raised a paw. "Midnight. It's Juno. Greetings! It's been a while. How's life among the gravestones?"

Midnight didn't move. Not at first. Then he blinked. Once. Slowly. His body went unnaturally still. His eyes filled with a glimmering silver fog.

He was no longer alone in there. Morticia was in control.

"Run," I whispered to Minnie.

Midnight launched at us with the elegance of a thrown dagger just as we bolted.

The cemetery came alive around us, the wind howling through twisted trees, and spectral lights flickering like vengeful fireflies.

My paws slipped on wet leaves as we darted between headstones. Minnie tripped over a decorative urn, flailed, righted herself, then ran straight into a wrought-iron angel and cursed so loudly even the dead stirred.

"He's faster than me!" she squeaked. "I'll get caught."

"He's faster than both of us. Keep up and watch your step."

Midnight surged after us. He didn't run. He glided. No sound. No panting. No hesitation. His claws shimmered with spectral flame, eyes glowing with Morticia's fury.

"Juno," he hissed. "You are not welcome here."

I tried to cast a blinding flare spell to slow him. It sputtered out and fizzled into an apologetic sparkle that looked like a fairy sneezing.

A vine shot out from a mausoleum and wrapped around my hind leg. I tripped and rolled.

Midnight landed beside me, murder mittens raised.

I ducked and threw up a shield. It was crooked, flickering, and humming. It caught one of Midnight's strikes but shattered on the second.

"Juno," he growled, "you're trespassing."

I backed up fast. A brief gust of magic surged through me, and I grabbed it and flung a stun bolt at Midnight.

It hit him in the chest, making him stagger. He snarled and shook it off like rain.

Minnie landed in a heap beside me. "Plan?"

"Survive until Midnight comes to his senses," I said. "I'll distract him. You escape."

Midnight pounced.

I turned to run, but he was faster. He collided with me mid-sprint, slamming me onto the cold, muddy ground between two tilted headstones.

His paw pressed hard against my chest, claws half-unsheathed, weight crushing. I couldn't move.

Minnie shrieked then vanished from sight with a thump. Had she fallen into an open grave?

"I'm not here to cause trouble," I wheezed. "I'm here to solve a terrible crime."

Midnight froze. Utter stillness. His head tilted slowly, like a statue turning to listen.

"He's sending a message to Morticia," Minnie whispered from close by. Yep, that definitely sounded like she was below ground.

A second later, Midnight opened his eyes, and the murderous look had vanished. "You have two minutes to explain why you broke into the cemetery. If Morticia doesn't like your answer, then I'm to destroy you both."

"If you could let me up, this will all make sense," I said.

He pressed down harder. "I can't do that. Explain yourself and be quick about it. Don't make me kill you."

"We're trying to solve a murder," I said. "Dr. Iona Wren's. I've reopened her cold case. We followed a suspect here, and we need to know why she was standing by a specific grave."

"Dr. Iona Wren." Midnight huffed out a breath. "That's a name I haven't heard in a long time. She's been gone for over twenty years, hasn't she?"

"Just about. And her murder was never solved," I said.

Midnight glanced at the hole Minnie was crawling out of. "You were her familiar. You disappeared because Angel Force thought you were involved in the murder."

"It wasn't me!" Minnie's voice sounded louder. "I'd have stayed hidden until I perished, but then I found out that Juno reopened the case, and I wanted to help."

"You didn't do it?" Midnight asked.

"I'd never hurt my witch." Minnie meowed her disapproval. "That's a terrible thing to say."

Midnight shrugged. "Who did you follow here?"

"Delphine Noxley," I said. "She was a suspect during the initial investigation."

"Huh! I remember she hated Iona. But she had good reason to," Midnight said.

"Because she lost her career thanks to Iona," I replied.

"Sure, that would be another reason to despise the woman, but..."

"There's another reason?" I asked. "Does that reason have to do with this cemetery?"

Midnight finally released his punishing grip on me and allowed me to stand and breathe properly. "Take me to the grave Delphine was at. I have a feeling I know which one it is, but I need to be sure."

Minnie took charge and led us to Vanhoff's headstone.

"I figured it would be this one." Midnight studied the engravings. "Don't you know who this is?"

"Only the basics. Iona briefly dated him, and then he died. Then she was killed," I said.

Midnight froze again and closed his eyes. They opened a few seconds later. "Just checking in with Morticia. She's intrigued enough to keep you alive. For now."

"That's gracious of her," I said. "Tell us about Vanhoff. What do you know?"

"You're right that Iona and Vanhoff dated. But before that, he was engaged to Delphine," Midnight said.

"Oh, I didn't know that," Minnie said. "Are you sure?"

Midnight glared at Minnie until she flinched. "Of course I'm sure."

"How did Vanhoff meet Iona?" I asked.

"I don't know the details," Midnight said. "Only that it didn't take long for Vanhoff to break off the engagement with Delphine and move on with Iona."

"He must have been serious about Iona to end an engagement," I said.

"Then he was an idiot. Iona was never serious about him," Minnie said. "It took me a while even to remember why the name was familiar. Men were just broomsticks drifting past in the breeze. Sometimes, Iona would grab one and take a ride, but then she'd get bored. She was too clever, you see. No one could compare. She needed someone to stimulate her mind, not just her... well, you know."

"This gives Delphine a perfect motive for wanting Iona dead," I said. "Not only did she lose her career after Iona reported her to the guild, but she lost her fiancé!"

"It's a great motive," Midnight said, "but you need to look elsewhere if you think Delphine is the killer."

"Why say that?" I asked. "I see no holes in the motive."

"Because ever since Vanhoff died, Delphine's been coming here every single wretched night. It doesn't matter what the weather's like."

"What does she do?" Minnie asked.

"Delphine sleeps on Vanhoff's grave."

I took a step back. "Every night since he was buried here?"

Midnight nodded. "Morticia hated it at first and tried to scare her off, but she understands. So long as Delphine doesn't cause a mess or disturb Vanhoff's grave, we tolerate her being here. I keep an eye on things."

I groaned. "That means Delphine was here when Iona was killed. Can you remember that night?"

"Of course not!" Midnight said. "That was too long ago. But I don't make mistakes. Delphine has been sneaking in every night without fail. Snow. Hail. Fog. It doesn't matter how nasty it is, or how many corpses are on the loose, she's here."

"Which was why that patient asked if she was taking a groundsheet and an umbrella," I said. "Delphine must lay the sheet over the grave before settling in."

Minnie sighed and slumped down. "Rats a million. I thought we'd solved it. Now what do we do?"

# Chapter 10

"That's disappointing." Sage's face loomed large in the snow globe. "Delphine was a perfect fit for the murder."

Minnie lay on her back, kicking her legs in the air as I finished relaying our latest lack of success in tracking our killer.

"There's no reason for Midnight to lie," I said. "On the plus side, we've got one less suspect to consider."

"But you're back to square one," Sage said.

"Square zero." Minnie sighed. "That's a place, right?"

"Not in my vocabulary," I said. "We have more suspects to check. And I vote for Lavender."

Sage huffed a breath, steaming up her globe. "Send her through. Let's find our killer."

**File:** #2001-1020
**Subject:** Quell, Lavender
**Interviewer:** Angel Sarah
**Location:** Quell Apothecary, Main Street, Badger's Haze

**ANGEL SARAH**: Please state your full name and magical occupation for the record.

**QUELL**: Lavender Miriam Quell. Potion maker.

**ANGEL SARAH**: You discovered Dr. Iona Wren's body. Can you explain what happened prior to that?

**QUELL**: Oh, stars, yes. It was an awful thing. I went to her place yesterday evening, probably around nine? No, definitely closer to half-past nine.

**ANGEL SARAH**: What was the reason for your visit that evening?

**QUELL**: To make her see sense, of course.

**ANGEL SARAH**: About what?

**QUELL**: That dreadful brooch. I told her it was cursed. It smelled cursed. Not literally, although sometimes cursed things have a sort of ozone-fried-elderflower scent, don't they? But it wasn't just that. It felt wrong. She said I was jealous. I said she was reckless. Then I slammed her door so hard I think I shook loose her ceiling beams.

**ANGEL SARAH**: And when did you return?

**QUELL**: This morning. Around half-past eight. I hadn't slept. Couldn't. You ever get that thing where your brain won't stop spinning and suddenly, you're reorganizing your entire spice shelf at three a.m.? Anyway, I felt guilty, and I wanted to clear the air. I even brought pastries. Apple turnovers. Iona always pretended not to like sweet things, but she'd eat those in two bites if no one was looking. I knocked. No answer. The door was wide open, which was odd. I went in, and there she was. On the floor.

**ANGEL SARAH**: You're certain she was alive when you left last night?

**QUELL**: Alive and furious. She could have knocked me out with one of those death glares of hers. So yes. Very much alive.

**ANGEL SARAH**: Neighbors report hearing a loud fight around 9:30 p.m. That fits with your account. Did anyone see you leave?

**QUELL**: I don't know. I wasn't exactly looking to be seen. I was fuming.

**ANGEL SARAH**: Did Dr. Wren ever mention anyone else causing her trouble? Clients, rivals, personal disputes?

**QUELL**: Oh, no. She helped everyone. The sick, the cursed, the magically deluded. She took on some real hard cases. Some of those people didn't always thank her. I know one man hexed her mailbox so all the parcels turned to slime. And don't get me started on those potion-purist lunatics who think anything liquid is the devil's work. She had enemies. They didn't bother her, though. Iona knew she did amazing work.

**ANGEL SARAH**: Did you notice anything unusual at the scene this morning?

**QUELL**: Was her poor body not unusual enough? No, sorry, that was flippant. Yes. The air felt wrong. Heavy and charged. And there was a movement under a chair.

**ANGEL SARAH**: What was it?

**QUELL**: A cat! Black and white. Scruffy. It looked like it had crawled through a firestorm and barely made it out.

**ANGEL SARAH**: That would have been Minnie, Dr. Wren's familiar.

**QUELL**: Oh! Of course it was. I should know that twitchy little glare anywhere. Yes. Minnie. She looked awful. All scuffed up, like she hadn't eaten or slept in days. I'm not a cat person, and can't see the appeal of having a cat familiar, but even I felt something seeing her like that. I don't trust cats, though. Do you? They're too quiet and clever.

**ANGEL SARAH**: I have no opinions on cat familiars.

**QUELL**: That's right. You don't have

familiars, do you? I'd have a dog or maybe a bird. Never a cat. I suppose if you could have one, you wouldn't pick a bird because you're so bird-like. I mean, all those feathers must take hours to groom. Do you use oil? Forget that. I don't have feathers. Don't you think it's weird?

**ANGEL SARAH:** What are you referring to?

**QUELL:** Minnie was Iona's familiar. She should have protected her, not hidden under a chair. It sat wrong with me. Don't you think that's wrong? It is wrong, isn't it? Or am I being foolish?

**ANGEL SARAH:** Are you making an accusation?

**QUELL:** Me? No. Never. I'm just saying cats are strange. They know things. They creep around, watching, and they always show up after something bad happens to enjoy the chaos.

**ANGEL SARAH:** Focusing on Dr. Wren, what contact did you have with the brooch or any of her enchanted items?

**QUELL:** None. I know my limits. Not like she did. That thing should never have been activated. I never liked it.

**ANGEL SARAH:** Why do you believe the brooch was dangerous?

**QUELL:** Oh, come on. You saw it. That kind of energy doesn't come from a garden-variety enchantment. It was built to do something unkind. I don't care what Crispin says about symbolic resonance or emotional imprinting for good. That thing wasn't just a mild magical item. It had been made with ill intent in mind. Remember, I was the first there, so I felt the leftover ick.

**ANGEL SARAH**: And you believe Iona knew about the brooch's power and used it anyway?

**QUELL**: I think she wanted to believe she could handle it. Iona always thought she could channel things others couldn't. She was brilliant, but sometimes brilliance makes people arrogant. Now, about you being a bird person...

**ANGEL SARAH**: Thank you, Miss Quell. Your statement is on record. Please don't leave the area. We may have further questions for you.


**Follow up**

Confirm Lavender Quell's timeline with any witnesses close to the crime scene.

Monitor Lavender. Her volatile nature, history with the victim, and access to

magical ingredients maintain her as a
high-priority suspect.

# Chapter 11

"Did Angel Force follow up after the interview with Lavender?" Sage asked.

"There's a note in here that the neighbors didn't see Lavender leaving Iona's house, so they couldn't verify timings," I said. "Minnie, do you remember her visit?"

"Lavender is hard to forget," Minnie said. "She has so much energy. She never sits still and talks twice as fast as anyone I've ever met. I definitely remember her visiting that night. She showed up with turmeric scones. Iona dropped hers on the floor so she wouldn't have to eat it. It was bright orange!"

"You remember that one irrelevant detail, but you don't remember what happened to Iona?" Sage asked.

"I remember the beginning of that evening," Minnie said slowly, looking hurt, "but then it all gets blurry."

"How convenient," Sage muttered.

"It's the truth!" Minnie said.

"Do you remember what time Lavender left?" I asked.

"I remember raised voices. Nothing much after that."

"Perhaps it was something Lavender did after she arrived at the house," I said. "If she cast a spell, it could have made you tired, so you weren't able to protect Iona."

"Was Lavender monitored by Angel Force?" Sage asked. "Her history with Iona suggests she should have been the prime suspect."

"I've got nothing in here to show the angels watched her," I said.

"They often argued," Minnie said. "It wasn't unusual. That was just how they were."

"Lavender was a potion mistress," I said. "She'd have access to magical ingredients most magic users wouldn't dare to touch."

"It wouldn't have been hard for her to give something to Iona or tamper with that hexed heart brooch," Sage said. "If she were skilled enough, Iona wouldn't have realized until it was too late."

"We should invite Lavender to Iona's house," I said. "Get her back to the crime scene. It could jog her memory or stir up guilt."

"Count me out. I'm never going back there," Minnie said.

"Have you really never been back since Iona was murdered?" I asked.

"Why would I? I lost everything in that hateful place. I don't want to dredge up those horrible memories." Minnie squeezed her eyes shut. "Please don't make me go."

"We don't have to. If you know where Lavender lives, we can visit her," I said. "Does she still have the store in the village?"

"No, that closed a while back," Minnie said. "It's a barbershop now and also sells those funny plastic smoking devices the youngsters like."

"So where do we find Lavender?" I asked.

"I haven't seen her around recently," Minnie said. "She's often foraging. She used to collect mushrooms and wild herbs, baking them into pies and cakes. Sometimes they worked, but often they just tasted strange and made you light-headed."

"I'd rather not hunt for her among the enchanted fungi of this village unless it's absolutely necessary," I said. "It never ends well when you tamper with fungi."

"Lavender was renting a room in the old hotel that got converted into studios," Minnie said. "That was a year or two ago, so she could have moved on, but we could start there."

"Let's do it," I said.

"Don't eat any food she offers you," Sage said. "It never ends well when you eat anything made by a volatile potion mistress with a liking for wild foraging."

"No matter how much my stomach grumbles, I'll refuse all offerings," I said. "You lead the way, Minnie."

Minnie took the long route to our destination, doubling back a time or two as if she'd gotten lost. "I don't want to draw any attention in the daytime," she explained. "People will look at me strangely when they realize I'm still here."

"It is strange," I said. "But it's a testament to how powerful your magic is if you can survive so long alone."

"It's more of an existence," Minnie said. "But at least now I have something to live for."

"You have no magic to rely on anymore?"

"I have some, but you never know what will spark out of my paw now I have no bond to tether me," Minnie said.

"I know that feeling," I replied. "Not being able to trust your own power is difficult."

"Here it is!" Minnie stopped by a faded back door leading into a large brownstone building. "This used to be the grandest hotel in Badger's Haze. It had a five-star rating, butler room service, the works. But as everything else faded, so did this building. It sat derelict for years, then someone bought it and converted it into smaller dwellings. I think they're all rented. This is where I last saw Lavender."

We had to wait a few minutes, but someone opened the back door and we snuck inside and headed along a dingy corridor. We made our way into an entrance hall, where there was an elevator with an out-of-order sign stuck on it and a flight of once-grand stairs. The paint was peeling, and the carpet had been removed, leaving the spiky carpet gripper behind.

"Look! We got lucky. Her name's on this post box," Minnie said. "She must still be here. Apartment 13."

"Lucky 13 for some," I said.

We headed up the stairs and located the apartment. I knocked, and the door was immediately flung open.

"Greetings! I'm Juno. You must be Lavender Quell."

"Oh, you're not who I was expecting." She peered past us, pushing long, dyed purple hair out of her eyes. "Is he ever getting here? I swear, that man doesn't know day from night."

"It's just the two of us," I said. "We're here to talk to you about Dr. Iona Wren."

"Don't know her. He should be here! Are you sure you didn't pass anyone on the stairs?"

"Could we come in?" I asked. "It won't take long."

Lavender stepped out the door and peered down the stairs. "Where is he? He's never usually this late."

I glanced at Minnie, and she shrugged.

"Are you waiting for someone important?" I asked.

"Of course! I can't leave until I get what I need." Lavender thumped her hands on her hips and kept looking down the stairs.

"Then why don't we wait inside with you?" I asked. "We'll keep you company."

"Oh. I guess." She glanced our way. "What did you want to talk to me about again?"

"Someone you used to know," I said. "Perhaps you recognize Iona's familiar, Minnie."

Recognition dawned in Lavender's eyes. "Um... that's impossible. You're dead!"

"I'm very much alive," Minnie said.

Lavender strode over and prodded Minnie in the side. "I'm sure you were dead. Didn't I come to your funeral? Or was that another familiar's funeral? There are so many deaths these days. Everyone just keeps dying and dying and more dying. It's this place, isn't it? It gets under your skin and sends you mad. It sent me mad a long time ago. Oh, you shouldn't use that word anymore, should you? What's the term now? Unstable? Unhinged? Crazy? It doesn't matter. It's all the same, isn't it?" She twirled her fingers on either side of her head.

"Could we come in?" I asked.

"I said yes! Didn't I? Who cares. Come in. I've made some hazelnut and lupin pancakes. They're delicious."

"I'm allergic to nuts," I said.

"And I'm allergic to lupins," Minnie glanced at me. "I don't know what a lupin is."

"Your loss. You're missing out. They're divine." Lavender led us along a cluttered hallway and into a studio where the bed and kitchen were contained in a single space. It was cluttered, with throw pillows and blankets scattered around. The scent of jasmine incense hung thick in the air.

"Who did you want to talk to me about again?" Lavender stood by the window, peering down into the street.

"Dr. Iona Wren," I said. "I know it's a long time ago, but you found her body."

"Iona? Of course. But that was another lifetime. Why are you asking me questions about her?" Lavender asked.

"I've reopened the case," I said. "And we're close to catching her killer."

That pulled Lavender's attention away from the window. "Oh! Wow. That's amazing. Who did it?"

"That's what I'm hoping you'll help us find out," I said.

"Doubtful." Lavender gripped her hands together and rubbed her palms from side to side. "Where is he? I must have something to calm my nerves."

"What are you anxious about?" I asked.

"Life. General living. It's all too intense these days. Everything is buzzing around and making noise. And you're here asking questions about someone who died years ago. It's hardly a surprise that everyone needs a little help these days just to breathe without thinking their heart is giving out."

"What extra help do you use?" I asked.

"My friend sells me stuff. It keeps me stable. I like that. He's a good friend, although his prices have gone up recently. I just wish he had better timekeeping. Lateness is so rude. It suggests my time isn't important. Although I have nothing else to do. That's not the point. You make an appointment and you stick to it."

"She's detoxing from something," I whispered to Minnie.

"Lavender was always the first to try new spells or substances," Minnie whispered back. "She'd sometimes walk around talking to invisible people. Having visions. That kind of thing. We were used to it."

"Then she's not a reliable witness," I said. "Was she this bad when Iona was alive?"

"Not so much. She's tipped over the edge. But it's no surprise, living here." Minnie grimaced as a large, hairy spider shot across the floor with a cockroach clamped in its fangs.

"My skin is itchy," Lavender said. "If he doesn't come soon, I'll have to go out and find something. But it's not safe out there, you know. Did you have any trouble getting here?"

"No trouble. We took the back route," I said.

"Good. That's good. Sensible. The last time I went outside, I saw three dragons and a unicorn. Oh, and there's an ogre who lives nearby, and he was smashing his club into anyone who got too close. It was terrifying.""It sounds awful," I said. "Perhaps you could focus on Iona just for a moment. It would take your mind off your friend's lateness."

Lavender shrugged, her nails dragging along her forearms. "Iona was never any help. She showed such promise when we first got to know each other, but she was as dull as everyone else."

"Do you remember finding her body?" I asked.

"Of course. You don't forget something like that, no matter how many memory wipes you attempt."

"Do you remember the argument you had with her the night she died?"

"It wasn't a standout fight. We always bickered, but that's the type of relationship we had," Lavender said.

"What did you argue about?"

"The thing that killed her! I said she had to destroy that nasty brooch because it was unstable. I feared it."

"What did Iona say about that?" I asked.

"I didn't give her much of a chance to talk. She laughed at me, and then I got angry. So, I left."

"But you went back the next day, and that's when you discovered her dead?"

"I wanted to say sorry for storming off. It was childish. I'm better than that."

"That was your only reason for going back?" I asked.

"Sure. Why else?" Lavender inspected the ends of her hair.

"You could have been the last person to see Iona alive," I said. "A hint of what happened just before she died could help us figure things out."

"How am I supposed to remember hints and clues after all this time?" Lavender asked. "I can barely remember what I did yesterday."

"Because she takes too many illegal herbs," Minnie muttered.

"There's nothing illegal if it comes out of nature," Lavender said. "I can't stay here a second longer."

"Where are you going?" I asked.

Lavender marched past. "He's not coming. He's forgotten again. He keeps doing this." She grabbed her coat and purse, along with a gardening kit.

"Do you have an allotment?" I asked.

She crouched and placed a hand on my head. "If you come with me, you must swear to keep this secret."

"What are we keeping secret?"

"Promise."

"Is it criminal?"

"Mildly."

"Will it get us in trouble?"

"Only if we get caught. And if you come with me, I'll show you exactly where I was that night after I bickered with my poor, dead friend."

I looked at Minnie, and she nodded.

"We'll join you," I said.

"Excellent. Hold on tight. I don't want anybody seeing me, so we're translocating."

Before I could protest, Lavender grabbed me and Minnie by the paw and cast her spell. The magic was erratic, spiky, and felt like someone was stabbing me with lots of tiny pins, but a second later, I was dumped on my back in the middle of an intensely strange-smelling herb garden.

"Climb out of that! You get too much on your skin and you won't be able to walk straight for a month." Lavender hauled me out of the herbs by my tail and dropped me onto a path.

I shook out my fur, feeling my skin tingling. "Where are we?"

"This is my second home." Lavender clapped her hands together. "Shush. You must not make a sound. We're not supposed to be here. People aren't supposed to know this place exists because it's so dangerous."

"Oh! This is the place with all the toxic plants banned from magical use." Minnie was looking around, although she hadn't gotten up from where she'd landed on her belly. "There are wards to stop people getting in here."

"Silly wards. They don't stop me. Not when I really want something to sample." Lavender danced along the path, her shears already out. She began snipping off pieces of herb and testing them on her tongue, then giggling.

"This is where you came after you argued with Iona that night?" I asked.

"Iona? We're still talking about her?" Lavender bent at the waist and peered at an intense blue bloom before sniffing it.

"Yes. Focus. You argued with Iona about the hexed heart, and then you left?"

"That sounds right," Lavender said. "Look at this twisted hellebore. I can boil this and make something extraordinary."

"After your argument, you came straight here?" I asked. "You didn't mention that when you spoke to Angel Force."

"Why would I?" Lavender said. "No one's supposed to visit here if they don't have a license to gather, and those aren't cheap. I needed something to calm myself down. I was worried about Iona, but also cross with her because she didn't listen to me. I snuck in here, took what I needed, and brewed it up."

"Then what did you do?"

She giggled again. "My brew was more potent than I realized. I fell asleep and woke up right here the next morning. I instantly thought about Iona and was full of regret. Although we often snapped at each other, I considered her a friend. So, I tidied myself up and went back to her house. That was when I found her on the floor. That brooch had killed her."

"Is there anyone who can confirm you were here that night?" I asked.

"Yes, always.""And who would that be?"

"The ravens. Or are they crows? I can never tell them apart."

"Birds were watching you?" I said.

"Not just any old birds, silly." Lavender turned and booped the end of my snooter. "Special birds. Magical birds."

Minnie groaned. "You mean Hester Gull's birds, don't you?"

"Yes! You clever little should be dead fluffy. Hester is almost as obsessed with this place as I am," Lavender said.

"And her birds are your alibi?" I wasn't sure that alibi would hold up during an interrogation.

"You're the most adorable creature I've ever met, but you're not clever, are you?" Lavender said. "Hester controls the birds. They act as her spies. They're everywhere. You just look up, and those beady eyes are watching. It's one of the other reasons I don't go out much. Anyway, that night, I came here, relaxed, and I remember seeing birds. Hester's birds. Always watching. Feathered little sneaks."

"Will they confirm they saw you?" I asked.

"Birds never lie. Or is that elephants?"

"Elephants never forget," Minnie said. "Hester's birds definitely lie. And swear! They're rude. And they peck. We don't want to go near them."

"They never peck me. I have the perfect alibi for that night." Lavender dangled a piece of greenery over my head. "Now, who wants to sample some of this twisted hellebore with me?"

# Chapter 12

"From what you've told me, Lavender is unstable." Sage's face was visible in the snow globe.

"This is the worst I've ever seen her," Minnie said. "There were rumors she'd pushed the boundaries when using magic to enhance her abilities, but I didn't realize she'd gone so far."

"She's smashed through those boundaries," I said.

"Maybe something went wrong the last time she was with Iona," Sage said. "She could have been using something dubious and lost control of her power, mistakenly infusing the hexed heart with warped magic. When Iona picked it up, it killed her."

"We need to double-check where Lavender was on the night Iona was killed," I said.

Minnie grimaced. "Please don't say what I think you're going to.""What's the problem?" Sage asked.

"Lavender told us Hester Gull's ravens were her alibi for that night," I said."Ravens and gulls?" Sage said."Just ravens," Minnie replied. "Hester Gull is a renowned bird whisperer, although she specializes in raven control. She lives in a spooky old tower on the edge of the village because no one wants her as their neighbor. She's obsessed with her birds. They're her only passion."

"Ravens as an alibi," Sage said. "That's a new one. I'm not a fan of birds, and from Minnie's expression, she wants nothing to do with them either."

"Hester has strong magic," Minnie said. "She manipulates the birds to do her bidding. It always made me uncomfortable. Ravens are intelligent birds and shouldn't be used like that."

"Is what Lavender said true?" I asked. "Hester uses the birds to spy on other villagers?"

"She used to. You don't see the birds around so much now," Minnie said. "Although you don't see many villagers around now either. Everyone keeps their heads down."

"That behavior won't have made Hester popular," I said.

"Before you go bird bothering, send me Hester Gull's interview," Sage said. "We may as well get up to date with what she saw that night."

I fiddled with the snow globe for a few seconds before I got it glowing and then sent through Hester's interview. "It's short and sweet. It makes for an interesting read and definitely gives Hester a motive."

Sage's image blurred. "I'll get back to you when I've read through it."

**Case File:** #2001-1020
**Subject:** Gull, Hester
**Interviewer:** Angel Sarah
**Location:** Gull's Aviary, Badger's Haze (interviewee refused to attend

an appointment at a more central location.)

**ANGEL SARAH:** Please state your full name and occupation for the record.
**GULL:** Hester Gull. Animist witch.
**ANGEL SARAH:** What was your relationship with Dr. Iona Wren?
**GULL:** Contentious. She testified against me at the Guild and cost me a teaching post. She claimed my birds were disruptive gimmicks and snooped. I claim she was afraid of any magic she couldn't control. We were not friends.
**ANGEL SARAH:** When did you last see Dr. Wren?
**GULL:** Two days before her death. She ignored me, and I ignored her. That's how it usually went. She thought I was a joke, and I knew she was a snob.
**ANGEL SARAH:** Where were you between 9:45 and midnight on October 18?
**GULL:** At home in my tower, feeding and tending my ravens. That's my routine every night.
**ANGEL SARAH:** Can anyone confirm you were there?
**GULL:** Not anyone you'd consider suitable. My birds will vouch for me, but I doubt you'd put that in your paperwork.
**ANGEL SARAH:** Did Dr. Wren have

enemies you are aware of?

**GULL:** Several. Lavender Quell comes to mind. They were close once, then they weren't. Lavender's unstable behavior is famous in this village. And Delphine Noxley loathed her. She lost her healer's license thanks to Iona's meddling. Neither will shed tears now she's dead. They'll most likely dance on her grave if they can get away with it.

**ANGEL SARAH:** Would you object to another animist witch speaking to your ravens?

**GULL:** If they try, they'll be torn apart. I'm saying no for their safety, not because I have anything to hide.

**ANGEL SARAH:** Do you have anything else to add?

**GULL:** Only this. You'll find many who resented Iona's power. She was gifted, but she wasn't loved. I hated her. Lavender always picked fights with her, and Delphine threatened her several times. Good luck finding out who did it. You'll need it with so many people happy that this day has finally come. Now, you need to leave. My birds are hungry, and they might mistake you for a snack.

**Follow up**

Verify Hester's stated alibi with her

ravens if there's a safe way to access them.
Maintain a watch on Hestor. There is a motive.

# Chapter 13

"Iona loved reporting people for infractions," Sage said. "First Delphine, then Lavender, and now Hester."

"She didn't do it because she enjoyed causing trouble," Minnie protested. "Iona expected things to be done by the book, and she knew powerful magic shouldn't be messed with."

"From Hester's interview with Angel Force, it sounds as if Iona considered Hester's abilities parlor tricks rather than important magic," I said.

"Iona was scared of birds," Minnie said. "She'd make me run outside and chase them away if any landed in the yard."

"That's no reason to belittle Hester's abilities," Sage said. "Controlling another creature takes skill."

"Most of us have an unreasonable fear about something or other," Minnie said. "And in Iona's case, it was anything with feathers."

I smirked. "How unfortunate for Angel Force."

"I don't think Iona disliked the angels," Minnie said. "And they usually keep their wings tucked away unless someone misbehaves."

"Before we get cold paws, let's visit Hester," I said. "We can check Lavender's alibi with the ravens and find out if Hester is keeping a secret she shouldn't."

Minnie hemmed and hawed for a few seconds. "Just be ready to run if the ravens turn feisty. You can never predict their mood. I blame Hester. When she's snappy, the birds are snappy, and that makes it unpleasant for all of us."

"You should take snacks for them," Sage said. "Snacks always make me feel better."

"They feast on roadside kill," Minnie said. "Anything from the size of a mouse up to the size of a small dog."

"I hope they don't look at us as if we're roadside kill," I said. "Let's head out. It looks like it's about to rain, and I want to avoid it if we can."

After Sage warned us to be careful several times, we left the library and headed into the gloomy day.

"When we get to Hester's, focus on Lavender as our reason for being there," I said. "We'll tell Hester we consider Lavender a suspect in this case and see if she has anything to tell us."

"And if she's involved, she'll try to pin Iona's murder on Lavender?" Minnie said.

"Exactly. Do you think Hester could have done it?" I asked.

"I don't remember seeing any ravens that night, but then I don't remember much," Minnie said. "Wherever Hester goes, there are always birds. They're her protectors and her eyes in the sky. She wants to make sure she's never caught doing things she shouldn't."

"Or she used them to make sure no one saw her killing Iona," I said. "We'll get her to open up by talking about Lavender and see if she lets anything slip."

It took twenty minutes to walk to the other side of the village, and as we grew closer to Hester's home, the path became uneven, and prickly brambles blocked our way.

"Hester is making it clear she doesn't want visitors." I hopped over a sharp pile of brambles.

"She says she's happy with her birds. Other people make her feel uncomfortable," Minnie said. "Some villagers used to get her involved in social events, but it got weird when she'd walk in with a flock of eye-pecking ravens squawking at everyone. The birds would strut around, stealing food, and pooping on things."

There was a sharp cry from overhead, and two large, sleek ravens took flight from a nearby tree and soared toward the solitary tower looming into view.

"She's got her guards out," I said.

"Her birds are always watching," Minnie replied.

A moment later, we stopped outside a faded yellow front door. Several ravens sat on top of the roof, their backs to us, waiting for us to be in the perfect position before dropping an unwelcome treat on our heads.

I dashed forward, knocked, and then ran back to avoid being splattered with something unpleasant.

Stomping footsteps marched toward the door, but it didn't open. "I'm not buying anything you're selling. Go away."

"Greetings, I'm Juno, and I'm here with Minnie," I said. "We have some questions for you."

"I'm answering no questions. Off you go."

"Hester, it's about Iona Wren," Minnie said. "I know you remember her. I used to be her familiar, and I need your help."

There was silence for several heartbeats before three bolts slid back, one after the other. The door inched open a crack.

"I thought you'd shuffled off to the other side a long time ago." Pale blue eyes stared out at us.

"I tried to. Several times," Minnie said. "But because Iona's death was never solved, I'm unable to move on. I must find out what happened to her."

"Why now?" Hester's eyes flicked to me. "What did you say your name was?"

"Juno. Angel Force has sent me here to solve the cases they couldn't crack."

"That's untrue. You're the banished cat!"

"Temporarily banished, and being put to excellent use while I'm here," I said. "May we come in?"

"No. I'm not able to help. We're talking about something that happened a long time ago."

"But you do remember it?" Minnie asked.

"Of course. It was the talk of the village. Iona getting herself messed up in a magic she couldn't contain," Hester said. "I tried to feel sorry for her, but she was hard to get along with."

"We're interested in a suspect Angel Force spoke to at the time of Iona's murder," I said. "Lavender Quell."

The door opened another inch, and I glimpsed Hester's long, straggly black hair and matching dark clothing.

"You think Lavender did it?" she asked.

"We've spoken to her," I said. "Her eccentric behavior raised questions."

Hester snorted a laugh. "Eccentric! That's one way to describe it. That woman has lost herself in the power of magical herbs. She thinks they won't harm her because nature grew them and gifted them to her. What nonsense."

"Lavender has a motive for wanting Iona dead," I said. "Do you think she did it?"

"Everyone thinks that the hexed brooch Iona was messing with caused her death. But after seeing what Lavender got up to on the night of the murder, I wouldn't be surprised if something else was involved."

"What was Lavender doing that night?" I asked.

Hester's eyes narrowed. "Sneaking about in the forbidden herb garden."

"You saw her there?" I asked.

"My birds did and reported back to me," Hester said. "You don't go in there if you want something mild and meek. Lavender was gathering seriously dangerous stuff."

"Do you think she used this seriously dangerous stuff on Iona?" I asked.

"I reckon she did," Hester said. "You've found your killer."

"That's fascinating. What time did you see her there?" I asked.

"She must have arrived around ten p.m. and stayed for hours. My birds said she was asleep when they left, and they patrol until dawn. They work in shifts, so they miss nothing."

"Are you sure about those times?"

"My birds are never wrong," Hester said. "Neither am I."

"Thank you for that information," I said. "You've given Lavender a cast-iron alibi."

"What are you saying?" Hester jerked back from the door. "Lavender isn't a killer? Why was she gathering those herbs if she wasn't using them to harm someone?"

"Lavender has a control problem with herbs," Minnie said. "When we met her earlier, she'd clearly enjoyed sampling nootropic delights. And she was waiting for more to show up."

"Well, perhaps I got things wrong," Hester said. "Or my timings are out. It was a long time ago."

"You said you and your birds are never wrong," I said.

"I... well, yes, I did say that. And I stand by it."

"So Lavender is innocent," I said. "Which means we're looking for a new suspect. Where were you when you got the news about Lavender poking about in the herb garden?"

"Where I usually am. Right here," Hester said. "That time of night, I'm always tending to my ravens. It's domestic bliss."

I dodged a falling dropping. "They are magnificent birds. Do you have a specific use for them?"

"Use?" Hester bristled. "I don't like your tone."

"You told us that your ravens watch. Do they watch all the villagers?"

"You make me sound like a snoopy sneak. I'm not. And I don't like you saying I am," Hester said. "Now, off you go."

"Could I confirm you didn't leave your tower that night?" I asked.

"Maybe I did, but I can't remember my movements from back then," Hester said.

Two ravens swooped past and called out, "Liar! Liar!" They circled the tower and then settled down, fluttering their feathers back into place.

"Why do your birds think you're lying?" I asked.

"Pay no mind to them. They've got a screw loose," Hester said.

"I suppose your birds watch you too," I said. "They make sure they're around to do your bidding."

"Bidding! I'm not their mistress!" Hester said. "They're free to come and go as they choose. They stay with me and choose to help me. We protect each other."

"Through their own free will or because you whisper to them?" I asked.

"Sometimes they're stubborn and need guidance. There's nothing wrong with helping them be logical and useful," Hester said. "This village doesn't want a pack of unstable ravens swooping around the place and stealing things."

Another large bird swooped past. "More lies! More lies!"

"You be quiet." Hester raised her hand, and the bird shrieked and shot off. "You two need to go as well. You're unsettling me, and that's unsettling my ravens. If I were you, I'd go back to Lavender and get her to confess. Or find out what she did with those herbs. Most likely, she stuffed them down Iona's throat and choked her to death."

"Thanks for the advice. We may come back again," I said.

"You better not, or my birds will see you off." Hester flapped her hand in our direction, then backed away and slammed the door shut.

I walked away with Minnie. "Hester was lying, wasn't she? She definitely uses those birds to snoop."

"Of course she does," Minnie said. "That's how she can afford this enormous tower. I don't know who for sure, but she's blackmailed several people, saying she'll keep their secrets so long as they give her money."

"Did she attempt that with Iona?"

"No! Iona didn't have any secrets worth being blackmailed over," Minnie said.

"Hester was quick to point the finger at Lavender," I replied. "Trying to shift the blame away from herself, perhaps."

Minnie nodded. "She has power since she can control so many ravens."

"Maybe enough power to order one of them to tamper with the brooch," I said. "A raven could have snuck into Iona's home and altered the magic. When Iona picked it up, it backfired and killed her."

"Hester has a motive too," Minnie said. "I know for certain Iona was the key witness in blocking Hester's guild application. And she openly mocked

Hester's ability to control the ravens. She called them bird tricks, and we'd joke about it."

"If one of Hester's ravens overheard you and Iona making fun of her, they'd have reported back," I said. "Hester would have been furious."

"It's a great motive, but we need evidence," Minnie said. "How are we gonna get it?"

I looked over my shoulder at the tower, where several ravens circled. "I need to come back and blend in with the locals."

# Chapter 14

"You should be able to do basic transmogrification spells by now." Sage looked shrewdly at me through the foggy snow globe. "You've been practicing old-school ways of doing magic for over a month."

"It's hard to go back to the basics when you've been an advanced practitioner for such a long time," I said. "We need to try again. If I can't disguise myself as a raven, I'll get no information out of that flock."

"You know what a flock of ravens is also called?" Sage asked. "An unkindness."

"I don't want to be a raven," Minnie said. "All those claws and that sharp beak. They're mean-looking."

"We have murder mittens and fearsome fangs," I said. "We're no less scary."

"But they fly!" Minnie hunched on the desk close to the snow globe. "And they're best friends with Hester. That means they have a mean streak. Like sticks with like."

"Hester was furious when those ravens yelled she was a liar," I said. "They know the truth about her, and I need to get the inside scoop. They could be the key to solving Iona's murder."

"Or they were mimicking." Sage flipped through a spell book. "Ravens copy other animals' voices. Maybe they heard Hester yelling at somebody else that they were a liar and were parroting it back."

"Ravening it back," Minnie said. "Get your birds right."

"You should've seen the look on Hester's face," I said. "And when she raised her hand, the ravens fled. They're terrified of her."

"Which means they're even less likely to talk to you," Sage said. "They don't want to be plucked and stuffed."

"They'll talk to me once I'm disguised as a respectable raven just passing through the village."

"Or, they'll see you as a threat to the flock and peck you to death," Sage said.

"It's a risk I'm willing to take to get to the truth," I replied. "Now find the kink in that spell we tried. The sooner I get back to the ravens, the better."

Sage grumbled to herself as she looked through a list of ingredients I'd need to turn into a raven. We'd been working on the spell since we came back from interviewing Hester, but it refused to stick for more than a few seconds.

"If we double the amount of fresh ivy, that could work," Sage said. "The resistance must be because you're weak. The spell doesn't want to stick to someone so magically blunt."

"I'm not that weak," I protested.

"You still haven't mastered a basic fire spell," Sage said.

"Wow! Really? I learned that when I was a kitten," Minnie said. "We all do, even those of us who aren't that good at magic."

"My circumstances are unique," I said. "I gifted my magic for the good of others. It was a noble sacrifice."

"One she doesn't stop bragging about," Sage said. "Try it and see if it works. Add the extra ivy, let it simmer for five minutes, stirring continually, and don't rush the process. Wait for it to turn dark green before cooling it and testing."

I attempted a salute with one paw, then got to work. Minnie had been trying to help but had knocked over several glass vials, so I'd confined her to the floor while we concocted the spell.

"How long has Hester had that raven flock?" I asked her.

"They come and go," Minnie said. "Although I always find one raven difficult to tell from another. They look the same."

"They probably say that about cats," I said.

"At least we have different colored fur," Minnie said. "They're all just sleek and powerful and dark."

"I saw one with a white wing feather," I said. "Perhaps I'll start with that one. The others may consider it an outcast, so it's less bonded to the flock."

"Whatever you do, don't hang about," Sage said. "There's no guarantee how long this transmogrification will last."

"It has to be at least an hour," I said. "We need to get back to Hester's tower, question the ravens, and then return before I change back."

"You could try flying," Minnie said. "That's a fast way to travel."

"No flying!" Sage said. "The wings are only for show. You'll have to walk and pretend you're injured or you're resting after a long flight."

"That won't seem suspicious," I muttered.

"If you attempt to fly and land on your head, they'll know you're a fraud," Sage said. "Keep stirring that spell."

I whisked the ingredients into a foamy cloud and didn't stop until the liquid turned dark green. I waited for it to cool enough to sip, measured out the correct amount, and drank the bitter liquid. A hot tingle ran from my booping snooter to my tail and back up again, racing through my body several times.

"It worked!" Minnie hopped up. "Oh yuck! You look awful."

I turned in a circle, admiring my sleek dark form. "I look like the perfect raven."

"Be the perfect fast raven," Sage said.

"I could come with you and watch from a distance," Minnie said. "Be your backup."

"That's not a bad idea," Sage said. "If Juno gets herself in trouble, she'll need help. We can trust you, can't we?"

"I'm trustworthy," Minnie said. "And I always look out for my friends."

"Just be careful," I said. "If you get caught spying on the ravens and then they figure out who I am, this won't end well for either of us."

"I'll be super stealthy. You won't even know I'm there." Minnie didn't look where she was going and walked into a bookshelf.

Sage rolled her eyes and sighed. "If you make it back in one piece, it'll be a miracle."

"You have such remarkable faith in me," I said. "We'll soon return with answers."

I hopped back and forth on my strange two legs, then hop-walked along with Minnie, who kept glancing at me and shuddering.

We hurried away from the library and headed to Hester's tower. The magic kept tingling, and every time it tingled, I checked to make sure my wings were still as they should be.

"Tell me if you see any white fur poking through," I said to Minnie.

"I'll whistle if I see anything odd," Minnie said. "You've got this."

We swiftly made it to the tower. Minnie speed walking, and me speed hopping. When we arrived, half a dozen ravens were lazily circling on the air currents.

"How do you say hello in raven?" I asked.

"Just squawk," Minnie said. "That's what they do. They're such noisy birds."

"You go hide before you're spotted." I shooed Minnie away, inhaled deeply, and let out a raucous cry.

It got the ravens' attention. They swooped lower, several of them zooming close to my head.

"You're not from around here," one of them said.

"I had an invitation to a gathering. I assume this is the right place since there are so many of you already here," I said.

"Whoa! There's a party happening, and we don't know about it?" One of the larger ravens thumped down beside me and flared his wings. "Righteous. Where's it happening?"

"A party? Sure. Isn't that what you're here for?" I asked.

"No. We live here. You're in the wrong place, my little dudette," another raven said, landing beside us. "We love to party. There's nothing fun going on around here. Not in this mangy tower."

"My mistake. I thought this must be the right place," I said. "I've been flying for hours, and I'm exhausted."

"We don't get a choice but to be here," the first raven said. "I'm Baldrick. And this is Darwin."

"Nice to meet you both," I said. "I'm Florian."

"Happy for you to visit," Baldrick said. "But you don't get to let your feathers loose here."

"You said you don't have a choice but to be here," I said. "Why can't you fly away? We could party together."

"We'd love to!" Darwin threw a wing over my shoulder. "But it's our job. We have to stay and get yelled at."

"You're compelled to live here?" I asked. "That doesn't sound fun."

"It's no fun," Baldrick said. "Our mistress is as mean as a stepped-on rattlesnake on the day everyone forgot her birthday."

"She must be powerful if you can't leave," I said.

"She's an animist witch," Baldrick groaned, flopping onto his back and kicking his feet in the air. "All she makes us do is work to gather everyone's secrets."

"Hush!" Darwin muttered. "Florian seems cool, but we don't know her."

"I'm not here to cause trouble," I said. "Just like you, I only want to party."

"Righteous," Baldrick said. "And we wish we could come with you."

"Maybe we can figure out a way to get you free," I said.

"Don't think we haven't tried," Darwin said. "Hester's always several steps ahead of us. And if we deceive her, we have to work twice as hard on half food rations."

"She's got her magic wrapped tight, and it's choking the life out of us," Baldrick added.

I acted surprised. "What does Hester make you do?"

"We spy on the village," Darwin said. "It's so boring."

"What are the villagers hiding?" I asked.

"Everyone has secrets," Baldrick said. "Hester blackmails the people who have something they're ashamed of. She's probably got dirt on everyone and has used it on about half of them."

"She takes money from them?" I said.

"Money, sometimes. Goods and services. Or she holds it over them. She likes that feeling of power," Darwin said. "What I wouldn't do just to kick back with a plate of bugs, a drink, and put my feet up. But no, we have to take shifts circling the village and seeing what everyone's getting up to. Day and night. It sucks."

"You're not talking about Hester Gull, are you?" I asked, pretending I'd just remembered her full name.

"Sure. You know her?" Baldrick asked. "Don't tell me, you used to work for her and you got free. How did you do it?"

"No, I've never worked for Hester," I said. "But rumors were going around years ago that she was involved in someone's murder."

"Wow! That would be quite some secret she's keeping if that's true," Darwin said. "Who did she off?"

"Someone called Iona Wren," I said. "She lived around here."

"Huh. The name doesn't ring a bell. But then, my memory's not what it used to be," Darwin said.

"It's because you eat too many of those dried goji berries," Baldrick said.

"That's not true! They're good for you!"

"Getting back to Iona," I said. "Have you never heard rumors that Hester was involved in Iona's murder?"

"Murder? Now, that is serious," Darwin said. "Hester's mean, but a killer?"

"She could be a killer," Baldrick said. "Don't you remember that raven who always talked back to her? The one who mimicked her voice? He'd disobey her orders and question them. One day, he disappeared."

"You think Hester killed him?" I asked.

"She probably baked him in a pie," Baldrick muttered. "She's always threatening to do that if we don't do what she tells us. She sings that nursery rhyme. The one about all the blackbirds being put in a pie, but she replaces blackbirds with ravens. It's creepy."

Darwin nodded. "Yeah. Gives me the chills when I hear her hum the melody. I don't want to be in a pie."

"Iona was murdered over twenty years ago," I said. "Were you around then?"

"Of course. Once you're bound to Hester, it's almost impossible to get away. A few ravens have done it. They've pretended they were sick, unable to fly. Some of them played dumb and kept forgetting things, so she... reassigned them."

"Reassigned them into a pie," Darwin grumbled.

Baldrick chuckled darkly. "Most likely. And then she ate it while watching us with her evil eyes."

"Hey, what's wrong with your feathers? They look furry." Darwin poked me in the side with his beak. "And you smell funny."

"Oh, it must be dust." I fluffed out my feathers, but suddenly, my wings felt wrong.

"No way! You smell like a cat." Darwin stalked around me. "Why would you smell like a cat if you're a raven?"

"I am a raven. I'm just here to party."

"Then why do you have a tail?" Baldrick asked.

I spun around, and sure enough, my marvelous white tail had sprung back into view. "When did that happen? The magic in this place must be strong."

"You're not a raven at all, are you?" Darwin jabbed at me with his huge beak.

There was a shrill whistle from nearby, coming far too late from Minnie.

"I can explain why I'm in disguise." I backed away. "I had to find out more about Hester. I'm investigating Iona's murder, and I need to know if Hester was involved."

"We may not like Hester, but we're loyal to her." Darwin hopped toward me with malevolent intent in his eyes. "And you've just deceived us. You're gonna pay for that."

I scuttled back, my two legs tangling with my tail. "Wait!"

Darwin let out a war cry squawk, and the flock exploded into motion.

Baldrick let out a sharp caw and launched into the air, wings snapping open like black sails. Darwin followed, shrieking a warning to the others. In seconds, half a dozen ravens wheeled above me, their eyes glittering with suspicion and feathers ruffled with fury.

"Get her!" one of them cried.

I tried to run, but I was too awkward on my skinny bird legs. Vicious claws closed around my wings and shoulders. Two ravens snatched me from either side, jerking me into the air with brutal force. My wings flailed uselessly, and my beak snapped shut as the wind blasted past.

"Put me down!" I squawked. "This is a misunderstanding! I'm investigating—"

"You're spying!" Darwin screeched. "We know a spy when we see one."

"Yeah, we are spies," Baldrick yelled.

A third raven dove in and pecked me hard between the shoulder blades. I yelped as pain flared along my spine. The flock surged upward, carrying me higher.

Branches whipped past below us. My feathers, unraveling under the strain of the unstable spell, itched and rippled. I felt my fur pushing through.

"She's shedding!" someone yelled. "She's turning back into a cat!"

"I said, put me down," I roared, but no one listened.

They climbed higher, talons digging into my sides.

Then Baldrick called, "Drop her."

I didn't have time to screech as the two ravens let go.

I plummeted through the air, spinning wildly, and slammed into the surface of a pond with a filthy splash. Freezing water closed over my head. Slimy weeds wrapped around my legs, and muck filled my mouth.

I thrashed upward, spitting out water and sludge, just in time to hear the mocking laughter of the ravens echo overhead as they circled me.

Darwin dove at me, and I ducked under the water, waiting for as long as my lungs would allow before bursting up for air, a rotting lily pad resting on my head.

The ravens were gone. And so was my dignity.

# Chapter 15

"Let me help you out of there."

I'd been flailing in the freezing, filthy pond water for what felt like hours—but was probably only a few minutes—before rescue arrived.

Dr. Greaves stood at the edge of the pond, concern on her face. She pushed up her jacket sleeves, revealing an attractive colored wrist tattoo, and held out a large stick for me to grab. "What did you do to Hester's ravens to make them so angry?"

I clung to the stick and allowed her to pull me to the safety of the bank. I flopped onto my belly, spitting out gross water and trying not to breathe too deeply, because my fur smelled foul. "Thank you for the help. The ravens disapprove of me searching for the truth."

"The ravens have the information you need to get to the truth?" Dr. Greaves dropped the stick and placed her hands on her hips. "Hester is known for her deception and trickery, as are her ravens. It wasn't sensible to tackle them alone."

"Only because she compels them." I forced myself to stand. "Stay out of splash range. I need to shake."

Dr. Greaves wisely backed up. I spent several seconds shaking like a common dog until my fur was no longer sodden and the worst of the pond sludge had been dislodged.

"Why did you think the ravens would talk to you?" Dr. Greaves asked.

"I went in disguise as one of them," I said. "I visited Hester earlier today and questioned her about her involvement in Iona's death. She took offense, but the ravens seemed to know more than she let on."

Dr. Greaves's eyes widened, then she burst into laughter. "So you went back as a raven? Well, I admire that, although it was dangerous. Those ravens are deadly."

"As I found out." I winced. "The back of my neck hurts where they pecked me."

"Oh, I didn't realize you were injured. Let me look." Dr. Greaves crouched beside me and gently parted my fur. "That's nasty. Do you have any healing spells?"

"I have little magic at the moment," I reluctantly admitted. "The transmogrification spell took it out of me."

"Really? That's a surprise. That's Magic 101. Well, not to worry. I know my way around healing spells. If you'll permit me."

"I'd welcome your help," I said.

Dr. Greaves gently placed her hands over my injuries, and warm pulses of healing light flickered over me for several minutes.

I sighed as the pain vanished. "Thank you. I'm not used to losing so easily. It's a humiliation."

"It's not your fault." Dr. Greaves stood and brushed off her damp palms. "Hester and her birds are known to be cunning. Did you get anything out of them before they turned on you?"

"Before they figured out I'd tricked them, they were helpful," I said.

"What did you learn?" Dr. Greaves asked.

"That Hester is blackmailing most of Badger's Haze."

"Oh, that's old news," Dr. Greaves said with a shrug. "May I take you home? You look exhausted."

"I'd appreciate that. I'm still living at the old library." It was only a twenty-minute walk, but just the thought of moving made me want to flop on my stomach and weep.

"That's on my way home." Dr. Greaves hesitated. "Would you like me to carry you?"

I was tempted. I dearly missed being carried or perched upon Zandra's shoulder. But I shook my head. It felt like cheating on Zandra if I let another magic user carry me.

"Let's just take our time," I said.

"As you wish." Dr. Greaves turned toward the library and walked slowly.

I staggered along beside her, glancing around to see if Minnie had gotten to safety, but there was no sign of her.

"How's it going with the investigation?" Dr. Greaves asked.

"I have leads," I said. "And I've ruled out some suspects. Hester gave Lavender Quell an alibi."

"That's good. Lavender is a troubled magic user. There's such a fine balance between using magic and having it exploit you. My fear is that Lavender has gone far into the realms of magical abuse. She may never find her way back."

"I got the same impression of her," I said. "Fortunately for Lavender, on the night of Iona's murder, she was scavenging for illegal herbs to fuel her addiction, and then passed out. So, she's out of the picture."

Dr. Greaves nodded. "Anyone else?"

"I'm still interested in Hester," I said. "Her ravens called her out as a liar when she said she was with them the night Iona died."

"That's interesting," Dr. Greaves said. "Hester is tricky. She has power, but she's a hoarder of all kinds of things, not just other people's secrets. I sometimes wonder if there's a hint of goblin in her ancestry. They love to hoard things."

"I've also spoken to Crispin, and he's still a suspect," I said. "He has no alibi."

"And he made the brooch," Dr. Greaves said. "I know Angel Force was interested in him when Iona died. It surprised me that they didn't convict him."

"They may yet," I said. "I'm still working my way through all the information."

Dr. Greaves glanced at me. "I wish there were more I could do to help, but it all happened such a long time ago. And with Iona's body turning to ash before I could complete my autopsy, I'm floundering to furnish you with anything that will move this forward."

"That was hardly your fault," I said. "The killer was sneaky and needed to destroy evidence. What better way than to turn a body into ash?"

"I'm still curious about what Iona did to displease someone so badly," Dr. Greaves said.

"The more I learn about Iona, the more I see she was a stickler for the rules," I said. "She reported anyone infringing on magical law."

"That's true. It didn't make her the most popular person in the village," Dr. Greaves said. "She must have picked the wrong person to report."

"Even if she was a pedant, she didn't deserve what happened to her," I said as we approached the library.

"You'll hear no protests from me," Dr. Greaves said. "I wish you luck with your continuing investigation. Although before you carry on, take a long soak to remove the swamp stench."

"That was a swamp the ravens dropped me into?"

"Swampish. It used to be a lovely pond," she said with a sigh. "We had all kinds of wildlife in there. But over the years, as with much of Badger's Haze, it's fallen into disrepair and slowly turned into a foul stink pool. A lot of people throw trash in there they can't recycle."

I shuddered, worrying about all the bugs and viruses I'd contracted.

"Get plenty of rest, and you'll be fine." Dr. Greaves reached to pet my head but then recoiled. "And take care. You're clearly stirring up trouble. You don't want to find yourself in over your head—literally or figuratively—again."

I thanked her once more and lurched up the library steps and inside. Once I'd reached the snow globe, I thumped my head against it.

A few seconds later, Sage appeared. "What happened to you?"

"The ravens happened," I grumbled. "Is Minnie here?"

"I haven't seen her since she went off with you." Sage peered at me. "What's that lump of green stuck to your side?"

"Swamp ooze." I flicked the offensive goo off with a paw. "Your spell didn't hold."

"That's not my fault," Sage said. "It didn't want to stick to you because your magic is feeble."

"This wasn't my fault!" I hissed at her.

"Let's blame the ravens then," Sage said. "Did you learn anything valuable?"

I swiftly updated her on my conversation with Darwin and Baldrick.

"So, you never got an answer about their thoughts on Hester killing Iona?" Sage asked.

"They questioned whether she could be a killer," I replied. "They clearly hate her and wish they weren't bound to her. But I believe they think she's innocent. If they'd seen an opportunity to accuse her of a crime and get rid of her, they'd have done so."

"Do you think Hester's innocent?"

"If she's misusing those ravens, then she's definitely not innocent," I said. "Hester feels like unfinished business."

"You can't go back there," Sage said.

"What am I supposed to do?" I asked. "We've been through all the suspects."

"There's one you've overlooked," Sage said.

"Who?"

"Minnie." Sage lowered her voice.

"It's not her."

"Check to make sure she's not listening in."

I glanced around. "Minnie must still be at the tower. She's probably making her way here. Or she's looking for me. She could have followed the ravens when they carried me off."

"Then that gives us time," Sage said. "Send me Minnie's statement."

"After everything she's done to help us, you still can't think it's her?"

"We've been around a long time. And although familiar-witch bonds are incredible, they're not perfect. The longer and older the bond, sometimes the more warped it becomes," Sage said. "We need to know if there was anything in Minnie's statement that made the angels suspicious of her."

I hated the idea that Minnie could be involved. But I had to keep an open mind.

I hunted through the file and extracted Minnie's statement. "I'll send it through, but I don't like this."

"You don't have to like it," Sage said. "You just have to accept the truth."

**Case File:** #2001-1020
**Subject:** Minnie
**Interviewer:** Angel Sarah
**Location:** 12 Rowan House, Ashen Row, Badger's Haze

**ANGEL SARAH:** Please state your full name and magical designation for the record.

**MINNIE:** Minnie. I'm a familiar. I was Iona's familiar. I mean, I am. No, was. I'm still getting used to what happened. It did happen, didn't it? I'm not making a mistake.

**ANGEL SARAH:** Iona is, unfortunately, dead. Please take your time. We're not unsympathetic to the loss of your witch when you were bonded. Where were you yesterday evening?

**MINNIE:** We'd had soup. Iona made soup that day. Parsnip. I don't like parsnips, but she said it was good for grounding. That was at lunch. Then... everything's hazy after that.

**ANGEL SARAH:** Were you with Iona in the hours leading up to her death?

**MINNIE:** I should have been. I always was, but she told me to go for a walk and said she needed quiet to work on something delicate. I think I went, like she asked. But then... I got lost? Or maybe I fell asleep? I don't know. I'm so sorry. Do you know what happened?

**ANGEL SARAH:** Did you see or speak to anyone that night who could confirm where you were?

**MINNIE:** I saw the librarian. Maybe? No. That was last week. Or maybe it wasn't. I'm not being helpful, am I?

**ANGEL SARAH:** What was your understanding of Iona's current clients or the magical objects she was working on?

**MINNIE:** She was messing with that brooch. The shiny one shaped like a heart. She wouldn't tell me what she was doing, but it didn't smell right. There was something bitter underneath the sparkle. She kept saying it was almost ready. I didn't like it. I told her not to touch it. I think I told her that. Maybe I imagined it. Can I see her?

**ANGEL SARAH:** Not yet. Did Iona express concern about anyone in particular? Was she worried about someone harming her?

**MINNIE:** She said someone watched her. But she always said that. And then she'd laugh and say it was probably the ravens. Hester sends her ravens out to spy. But last week, Iona was jumpy, and she burned a whole batch of calming sage. I remember the stink. And she told me not to answer the door.

**ANGEL SARAH:** Do you recall the moment you found her dead? You were in the same room as Iona when Lavender arrived.

**MINNIE:** Lavender? I... not really. I kept looking at her and then closing my eyes and hoping things would change. I kept thinking she'd walk in and scold me for knocking over a potion vial. I did that sometimes because I don't see so good. I... I don't understand how she's gone.

**ANGEL SARAH:** Thank you, Minnie. We'll review this statement and follow up if necessary. And I'm sorry for your loss.

## Follow up

Minnie doesn't present as hostile or malevolent. However, her magical bond with the deceased may have caused residual instability or trauma-induced memory suppression. While there is no evidence of direct involvement in the incident, Minnie's emotional volatility, along with the absence of an alibi, means she can't be ruled out. Her magical aptitude and historical record as a familiar have been stable, but as with all long-term bonds, psychological entanglement may have caused atypical behavior.

Do not re-interview at this stage. Emotional state is fragile. Flag for follow-up if new magical evidence or witness statements contradict or clarify Minnie's account.

Maintain provisional suspect status pending resolution of an alibi.

# Chapter 16

"After reading that, do you still trust Minnie?" Sage asked.

I didn't reply for a full minute, the silence stretching between us as my gut churned. "I only skimmed Minnie's statement. It's clear she was distressed after Iona died."

"There was more than distress in that statement," Sage said. "Minnie felt neglected, and she wanted to win Iona back."

"From everything we've learned, Iona was obsessed with her work," I said. "Perhaps she lost focus on Minnie."

"It wasn't just her work. It was that hexed heart brooch," Sage said. "There must have been something in that brooch that influenced Iona, dragged her attention away from everything else. That would have impacted Minnie and their bond. Maybe even warped it and made Minnie desperate to fix things."

"You think she tampered with the hexed heart and it backfired?" I asked.

"It could have been a mistake," Sage said slowly. "Minnie never meant to kill her witch, but something went wrong."

"If she did it, and I'm saying a big if, it must have been an error," I said. "We all know if the witch we're bonded to dies, we fade away, too. It could take months or years, and a few are lucky enough to find someone new to bond with, but eventually, most of us die. It's the price you pay for finding a perfect match."

"Minnie found that match, and she refused to let it go," Sage said. "She was heartbroken and full of anger over what was going on with Iona. And she did something about it. Maybe she hoped to break the hexed heart, but instead, she infused it with too much power."

"And Iona paid the price." I looked down at the file. "Maybe I have been naïve with Minnie. I've barely paid her attention when thinking about suspects. But if she is the killer, then I'll get a tattoo."

"Hah! I'll hold you to that," Sage said. "It's time you learn the truth. We could have been making friends with a killer all this time."

I grimaced. "What do you have in mind?"

***

"I don't feel good about this." I crouched near the snow globe so only Sage could hear me.

"It doesn't matter if you feel good or bad," she whispered. "You have to do this. You can't overlook Minnie just because you formed a friendship."

"You sound jealous."

"I'm not jealous. I'm concerned," Sage said. "You're lonely in Badger's Haze, and you want a friend. No one wants to give you the time of day, and now Minnie shows up. Don't tell me you've already forgotten what Roland did to you."

"The fake Roland. Not the real Roland," I said.

"Even the real one hasn't bothered to come round much since you got him out of that grave."

I huffed out a breath. "After everything we did for him, he could at least have sent over a hamper full of fresh fish."

"He's probably getting his life back together," Sage said. "But that's beside the point. I've suspected Minnie since you opened this case. She was there when Iona was killed, yet she remembers nothing about it."

"Because Minnie was blasted with incredibly powerful magic that messed with her memory," I muttered.

"Or she's using that as an excuse, and she can remember exactly what happened," Sage said. "She's sticking close to you to make sure you don't get to the truth. And when you do, what do you think she'll do?"

"Minnie's too clumsy to hunt me," I said.

"If she wants to silence you, she'll do it," Sage said. "She managed it with Iona, so Minnie won't be afraid to test your limits. Such as they are."

"My magic is slowly getting better," I said.

"When was the last time you brewed a potion that didn't go wrong at least once?"

I wrinkled my booping snooter. "It's been a few days."

"It's been twenty days," Sage said. "You have to practice the old ways daily. It's not just a matter of tapping into your innate abilities and having it all go poof. Brewing potions takes time. And brewing ones that actually work takes even longer."

I heard footsteps approaching. "That must be Minnie. Just stick with the plan and let me do the talking."

Sage fell silent just as Minnie ambled into view."Hey, you're up early. Couldn't sleep?" Minnie asked.

"I keep thinking about what those awful ravens did to me," I said. "And my fur still smells strange."

"You do whiff. You should have another bath."

"There's only cold water in this place," I said. "I stuck it out as long as I could. Perhaps the hot water in Iona's house still works."

"I wouldn't know, but I doubt it. Everything must have been shut off by now."

"Did no one ever want to move in? Turn it into their own place?"

"I suppose when something so terrible happens in a home, it gets a reputation," Minnie said. "Even though I never go there, I've heard the whispers about it being haunted by an unhappy spirit."

"Could that be Iona?" I asked. "If her ghost is around, we could talk to her and see if she remembers what happened that night."

"It won't be Iona. If she were around, I'd know," Minnie said firmly."But you don't go to her house," I replied. "Iona might be trapped there and desperate to see you. She'll be so confused, thinking you've abandoned her."

Minnie frowned. "She's not there. If the spirit of my bonded witch was still in Badger's Haze, I'd feel her."

"Fair enough," I said, sensing this wasn't the route to convince Minnie to act. "What plans have you got today?"

"I thought we were spending the day together. Haven't we got more people to question?"

"We've been through all the suspects and reached dead ends," I said.

"What about Crispin?"

"You think he did it?" I asked.

"He made the brooch." Minnie cocked her head. "And then there's Hester. The ravens didn't support her alibi for the night Iona died."

"True, but I don't want to tackle Hester again just yet. I've yet to recover from the first encounter."

Minnie chuckled. "I don't blame you. I chased after the ravens as fast as I could, but lost them. I'd have helped you out of the swamp pond if I'd known that's where they dunked you."

"I figured as much." Although I wasn't so sure of anything Minnie told me anymore. Had she deceived me all this time, and I'd fallen for it because I needed a buddy?

"So, we go back to Crispin and dig some more?" Minnie suggested.

"I think I'll go over the case file again," I replied. "I want to make sure I've missed nothing."

"What do you think you've missed?" Minnie hopped onto the desk, almost missing her footing and having to scramble up at the last second.

"I won't know until I find it," I said. "Why don't you head out on your own today?"

Minnie looked appalled at that thought. "And do what? Everyone in this place thinks I'm dead, or that I killed Iona. It's hardly safe for me to amble about making idle chit-chat."

"Then stick to the back alleys like you always do," I said. "You must get bored being stuck in here with me, Sage, and the ghosts."

"Nothing is boring about you two," Minnie said. "It's good to have other familiars to talk to. Well, I know I'm not a familiar anymore, but you know what I mean."

I glanced at Sage, who'd remained silent.Sage glared at me, the sharp look in her eyes warning me not to do anything foolish or forget the possibility that Minnie was a killer.

"At least head out and listen to some conversations," I said. "See what people are saying about me poking around in Iona's case. Our actions must have gotten the locals talking, so someone might let interesting information slip."

"You're more optimistic than I am," Minnie said. "But I can do that. I need to find a new place to get food. The old store has run out of my favorite brand of kibble."

"By obtain, you mean steal?" Sage asked.

"I have no money. Iona's not here to pay for anything. And technically, I'm not supposed to be alive, so what else am I supposed to do?" Minnie said.

"No judgment. A cat has to eat. We hear you," I said. "I've been scavenging the stores ever since I got here. The library pantry was pitifully bare."

"I'll see if I can get you something, if you like," Minnie said.

"I would like, thank you. I'm fond of salmon," I said.

"I'll see what I can find." Minnie hopped off the desk, stumbled over her paws, and then headed off, her tail up.

"I feel guilty, but that should keep her busy for a while," I said.

"And you too," Sage said.

"What do you mean?"

"You need to follow Minnie!"

"But she's going to get us food."

"Don't believe that. You can't let her out of your sight. After we read her interview, it's clear she's unstable."

"That's unfair. Minnie was lost in grief when she gave her statement."

"We've talked about this. You must keep a close eye on Minnie. This isn't the first time she's skipped out. Where did she go after Iona was killed? You'd never leave Zandra if she were murdered. And I'd rip the moon from the sky to find anyone dumb enough to hurt Vorana."

"Maybe the magic messed with her," I said. "Or she panicked and realized Angel Force thought she was guilty."

"Maybe she is guilty!" Sage jerked her chin forward. "Follow her. See what she gets up to."

It felt wrong to skulk after my new friend, but I couldn't overlook Minnie's involvement.

After grumbling a few more times, I hopped off the desk and headed out to see which way Minnie had gone. I took the back route, assuming she would have used it, and quickly caught sight of her black tail. She wasn't hurrying, simply moseying along the alleyway, stopping to sniff at something now and again.

She carried on for five minutes. But then, unexpectedly, she came to a fork. Rather than turning right, which would have taken her to the stores, she turned left, which was the route out of the village.

My pace increased so I wouldn't lose sight of her. Where was she going?

Minnie's movement was more purposeful as she strode along, her head up.

We kept going for another ten minutes, and my heart skipped as I realized where we were headed.

Minnie had lied. She was going to Iona's house.

I hoped I was wrong, but with every pawstep I took, the truth grew clearer.

Eventually, Minnie paused, climbed a stone wall, and jumped over the top, disappearing out of sight.

That was the boundary of Iona's house.

I huffed out my frustration as I sped closer. Rather than following Minnie over the wall, just in case she was waiting on the other side, I walked to where a double gate hung open.

I peeked around the edge. Minnie walked toward the house and then around the side. I dashed after her and was just in time to see her slip through an open window.

"You rotten liar," I muttered under my breath as I made my way toward the house. "I have terrible taste in new friends." Well, I did here, anyway. First Roland, and now Minnie. Both had deceived me. At least Roland had a decent excuse. But what could Minnie say when I called her out on her lies?

She'd said repeatedly she'd never visited Iona's house because there were too many bad memories. And there she was, bold as brass, sneaking inside to do who knows what.

What else had she lied about?

I took a risk and hopped onto the window ledge. I looked in on a messy study, untouched for years. The house must have been left to fall into disrepair after Iona died.

There was no sign of Minnie in the room, so I jumped down and took a few seconds to get my bearings.

There was a small thud in the hallway that made me freeze for a second. I dashed behind a chair and waited to see if Minnie would come in. When she didn't appear, I crept toward the door and poked my head into the hallway.

There was another clatter as something hit the floor.

What was Minnie doing in here?

I crept along, my belly low to the floor, until I arrived at the room where the noises came from.

Minnie sat on a workbench, a variety of objects sitting in front of her. Most of it was jewelry. Minnie had her paws pressed on a thick gold bangle, and a faint glow came out of the red gem in the bangle's center.

After a few seconds, she sighed and kicked the bangle away. "Useless. None of you are any good. Why can't you be as good as the heart?"

I sucked in a breath. Was she talking about the hexed heart? Had Minnie used it?

She leaned over the workbench, digging into open drawers and kicking things out. "Gah! It's all useless. Everything here is useless. What am I supposed to do now?"

I stared in horror as Minnie kept thumping the pieces of jewelry and artifacts on the workbench. Some of them glowed for a few seconds, but whatever magic had once been in them was faded.

Was this how Minnie had used the hexed heart brooch? Had she absorbed some of its energy and needed a magical fix from something else to keep going?

Most importantly, had Iona caught Minnie taking magic from the brooch and confronted her? They argued, and Minnie killed Iona to silence her and keep the brooch and its power to herself.

Or it was an accident, and she didn't realize how much power she'd taken from the hexed heart. Minnie didn't know her own strength and destroyed her bonded witch. If that were true, she'd feel terrible.

My heart hardened. Even if it had been an accident, if Minnie was behind this, I had to stop her and make her pay for her crime.

I stepped into the room, and my movement caught Minnie's eye.

Her head shot up, and her mouth dropped open. "Juno! What... what are you doing here?"

"Finding Iona's killer, I fear," I said. "It was you, wasn't it? All this time, you've been lying to me."

"Of course not. I've been telling you the truth!" Minnie kicked the jewelry back into a drawer. "I was just... looking around."

"You didn't tell the truth when you said you never came to Iona's house because of all the bad memories," I said.

Minnie's nose twitched. "You wouldn't understand."

"Try me."

"You think I'm misusing magic—"

"I just watched you do exactly that!"

"Not true. There's barely any magic here to misuse."

"You misused the hexed heart, though, didn't you?" I asked. "You got caught taking power that didn't belong to you. That was why you silenced Iona."

"That's not what happened." Minnie hopped down from the workbench, her hackles lifted.

"So why are you here?" I took a step back, realizing how little magic I had, and no clue how strong Minnie actually was.

"I'm looking for clues!" Minnie said. "You seemed so surprised that I hadn't come back here, so I realized I needed to help more. It's important to be useful."

"I don't believe you," I said. "I was convinced you wanted to find the truth about what happened to Iona, but you already know it."

"Stop saying that! I had nothing to do with Iona's murder," Minnie said.

"You were here when she was killed!"

"And I was blasted with magic, so I don't remember a thing about that night," Minnie said.

"Maybe you've lost the memory of actually killing Iona, too," I said.

Minnie paused. "I'd never forget that."

"With a powerful enough spell, you might," I said. "Minnie, you're in trouble. You need help."

"Not from you! And you're not pinning Iona's murder on me just because you've failed to find out who did it."

"You've been taking power that doesn't belong to you. I understand why. You've lost the familiar bond, and you're desperate to stay alive. But not like this. It's wrong."

Minnie hissed and launched at me.

I ducked, thinking she was about to attack, but she flew straight over my head and out the door.

I scrambled to my paws and took off after her. "Minnie, stop!"

She darted through a half-open door, and I followed her. She leaped from a table to a windowsill, then launched through an open window into the overgrown garden.

I continued the chase, gathering what magic I could. Green sparks flew from my paws and struck the tangle of ivy beneath the window. It surged forward, snaking around her hind legs and slowing her escape.

Minnie hissed, twisting in mid-air, and blasted the ivy apart with a pulse of raw energy. The force sent her tumbling, but she recovered quickly and kept running.

I raced into the garden. "You don't have to run. Stop and talk to me!"

She didn't reply, just bolted through a sagging wooden archway and into the remains of the old conservatory.

I charged after her. "I thought we were friends!"

She skidded to a stop, whirled, and flicked her paw toward a wooden crate. It rose into the air, surrounded by a faint glow, and launched at my head.

I ducked and conjured a glimmering dome just in time to deflect the crate.

"I didn't mean to lose control!" Minnie shrieked, her voice cracking with desperation.

I inched closer. "Over what? Your power?"

Minnie's eyes flashed with panic. "You don't understand. I needed the magic. I needed her back." Her breath was ragged.

I followed slowly, my heart thudding, and magic prickling at my whiskers. "Minnie, please. Just stop. Let me help you."

"I can't," she whispered. She reared back and slammed her paws into a bookshelf, sending a wave of magic through it.

The whole thing groaned. For a second, nothing happened. Then it tilted. She darted past as the shelf toppled, books raining down in a heavy, thundering mess.

I tried to leap clear, but falling volumes slammed into my stomach and shoulder, and the shelf crashed down, pinning my tail and half-burying me in a heap of dusty tomes.

I wheezed, struggling to shift the weight without losing the tip of my glorious tail. By the time I'd dragged myself free, Minnie was gone. I lay on my side, panting, my stomach aching. But it was the ache in my heart that hurt the most.

Sage had been right all along. Minnie was our killer.

# Chapter 17

"You need to get better with your healing potions." Sage peered at me through the snow globe. "You could have treated yourself without limping back to the library and patching yourself up."

"If that's your idea of sympathy, you're doing a terrible job," I muttered through gritted teeth as I soaked a bandage in a poultice Sage had helped me concoct and rested it over another bruise.

"Things have changed for you," Sage said. "You can't just flick a paw and have everything perfect."

"Things were never perfect," I protested. "But they were a lot better when I had access to my power."

"You could have more power if you—"

"I know. If I practice. But it takes too long to use the old ways to conjure magic."

"Everyone who first learns anything is terrible at it," Sage said. "You don't imagine the world's greatest guitarist picking up a guitar and knowing what to do. It would have taken them decades of hiding in their bedroom as a spotty-faced teenager, plucking away at strings while they annoyed their parents and ignored their homework."

"I'm more mature than a teenager," I said.

"Sometimes that's debatable. And I know why you're really so grumpy."

I applied the last piece of soggy poultice and slid down onto my belly, resting my chin on the desk. "Why's that, oh wise one?"

"Because you've discovered Minnie, who you thought was on your side, is our killer."

I sighed heavily and closed my eyes for a few seconds. "I got her completely wrong. What is it about the familiars in this village? Do they all turn on their magic users?"

"You've met two familiars who have done that," Sage said.

"It's a pattern."

"It's a coincidence! I was always suspicious of Minnie, though. You were the one with the blinkers on."

"Am I not cut out for this anymore?" I asked. "When I was with Zandra, we could solve any case given to us. I almost failed to figure out what was going on at the whispering well, and Minnie easily hid her true nature from me. Perhaps I need to hang up my private investigation license. Do something more sedate."

"First off, you don't have a private investigation license, you just poke your nose in places people don't want you to. And second, what would you do that's more sedate? Jigsaw puzzles? Gardening?"

"No, I wouldn't want to get the dirt stuck in my claws," I said.

"You're not made for sedate. You never were and you never will be," Sage said. "And don't think all this morose talk is letting you off our bet."

I winced. "What bet would that be?"

"You haven't forgotten. We made a deal. If you found out Minnie was guilty, then you'd get a tattoo."

"That was said off the cuff. I never meant it," I said.

"I did. And you agreed, so you're getting one," Sage said.

"I have nowhere on this perfect body for a tattoo to go. And I'm not shaving off a patch of my fur."

"You don't have to. Get one done on a paw pad."

"My toe beans are sensitive!"

"It only needs to be a small one. But a deal is a deal."

"I didn't think you were serious."

"I wanted to make sure you were," Sage said. "You were convinced Minnie was innocent, and I wasn't."

"There's no need to sound so smug," I said.

"I have every right to be." Sage's eyes glimmered with mirth. "You could get a tattoo of a tiny hellhound."

"I'm not keen on that idea," I said. "I've nothing against hellhounds, but they need something much more impressive than a tiny tattoo to represent them."

"A butterfly is too cliché," Sage said. "How about a witch's cauldron?"

"How about nothing? And you stop being mean," I said. "I have a serious injury. I was lucky to survive Minnie's vicious attack."

"More like the bookshelf's attack," Sage said. "Minnie probably knocked it over by mistake."

I shook my head. "I still can't believe she did it."

"Yeah, that's bad news," Sage said. "Once you're healed, you need to make a plan about what to do with her."

There was a loud rat-tat-tat at the main library door.

I tensed. If Minnie was planning to skulk back in here, she'd never knock to announce her arrival.

"Are you expecting company?" Sage asked.

"I didn't invite anyone over. There's no point. Every time I issue an invitation, I get ignored or yelled at." I struggled down off the chair and then eased my way onto the floor.

The noise came again. Whoever was outside wasn't leaving.

I limped toward the door and pressed my paw against it. Although my magic was weak, I sensed no malevolence on the other side. But I got a strong smell of hot feathers.

Inching the door open, I peeked through the gap. Baldrick and Darwin stood on the other side, hopping from foot to foot.

Baldrick jumped up and down when he saw me and flapped his wings. "Hey! You survived the swamp drop. Excellent."

"No thanks to you," I grumbled. "If you're here to cause me more harm, then I suggest you scurry away before I set the library ghosts on you."

"Oh no, dudette, you've got it all wrong." Baldrick stepped aside and gestured for Darwin to move forward.

Darwin held a small leather notepad in his beak.

"What have you got there?" I asked. "And will it explode if I touch it?"

"Sorry we dunked you in the gross goo," Baldrick said. "We have issues with rage. It comes from living with Hester. We got het up over you deceiving us, and we let our worst instincts take over."

"You're apologizing?" I didn't hide my surprise. I'd assumed I was now on the ravens' hit list, so I'd need to hide from them whenever I left the library.

"This is a big apology," Baldrick said. "We should have asked you why you disguised yourself, rather than attacking. We're trying to be better ravens, but it's not always easy when we have such an awful role model."

Darwin spat out the notepad and shook his head. "Hester brings out the worst in us."

"You need to find a way out," I said. "What's in the apology notepad?"

Baldrick squawked out a laugh. "That is Hester's little black book. And it's not full of her sordid dating history."

Darwin hacked out a coughing, raspy cackle. "If it were, it would be blank."

They wing high-fived each other.

"It's a list of all the people in Badger's Haze Hester blackmailed or is currently blackmailing," Baldrick said.

"Although, as you'll see," Darwin added, "the offerings she's getting these days are less than they used to be. People have barely anything, but she still takes from them."

My eyes widened, and I reached for the notepad.

Darwin stepped on it. "We really are sorry. You didn't swallow any swamp water, did you?"

"Only about a gallon. I can still taste it at the back of my throat."

"Jeez, that sucks. Sorry, dudette," Baldrick said. "Although you were lucky that you landed there. When we yelled for you to be dropped, I was aiming for solid ground."

"Then I'm glad this is such a significant apology gift," I said. "I could have broken bones."

"Yeah, that would've been lousy," Darwin said. "Anyway, have fun with the book."

"Wait. Won't Hester notice this is gone?" I asked.

"We're always messing her stuff up, so we've got time before she figures out it's gone for good," Darwin said.

"I'll look through it and get it back to you," I said. "I don't want you to fall under Hester's spite. I imagine her punishments aren't gentle."

"We're used to it," Baldrick said. "Happy reading."

They took off and flapped away into the gloom.

I hurried back inside the library with the notebook clamped between my teeth, heaved myself onto the desk, and dropped it next to the snow globe where Sage waited.

"Who was it?" she asked.

"The ravens who dumped me in the swamp pond," I said. "They felt bad, so they stole Hester's blackmail list."

"Is that it?" Sage peered at the notepad.

I was already flipping slowly through the pages. "Yes. There are a lot of names in here. Some I recognize."

"What kind of thing was Hester blackmailing them about?"

"Dubious business dealings. A few affairs of the heart. Some financial shenanigans. It's all listed here. Who she blackmailed, what she was blackmailing them about, and how much she made off of them."

"Hester is after their money?" Sage asked.

"Mainly, although there are a few items of furniture and jewels in here. Some rare magical items, too. Favors as well."

"What did she have on Iona?" Sage asked.

"Let me get to the end of the notepad. I haven't seen Iona's name yet," I said.

There were over a hundred names written down, so it took me time to work through Hester's scrawling words.

"Found Iona yet?" Sage said.

"That's odd. Let me check. I must have missed Iona's name." I started from the back page and worked through each one slowly. When I got to the front, I frowned. "We have a problem. Hester never blackmailed Iona. There's no record here that they were ever involved in that way."

"That's not great news," Sage said. "There's a motive if Hester was blackmailing Iona. They had a disagreement, and Iona decided she no longer wanted to be blackmailed."

"Or she threatened to report Hester to Angel Force," I said. "But if Hester never had a secret on Iona..."

"Then Hester is innocent!"

I was silent for a moment as I triple-checked the notepad. There was no mistaking it. Hester had nothing over Iona.

"You know what this means," Sage said.

"It makes it even more likely that Minnie is our killer," I replied with a grimace.

"That's right. And now, you have to figure out how to find her before she vanishes for good."

After a decent night of rest, I felt better. Mainly thanks to the poultice I'd brewed up, with Sage's help.

Following an uninspiring breakfast of stale kibble, I settled in front of the snow globe. Sage was stuffing her face with a delicious plate of smoked salmon and scrambled eggs dripping with butter, which I pretended to ignore.

"I'll try a location spell to find Minnie," I said. "I doubt she's left Badger's Haze. If she's still here, I'll be able to track her."

"You do that," Sage said around a mouthful of food. "Then I'll tell you about my research."

I blocked out her munching, rested my paws on a blanket Minnie had slept on, so I had a personal connection to her, and cast the spell.

A small ball of light flickered into existence. It wobbled for a few seconds and then vanished.

I cleared my throat, flexed my paws, and tried again. Every time, the location spell botched.

"That's either your dodgy magic failing or Minnie is masking herself," Sage said.

"I can achieve a basic location spell!" I said.

"Which means Minnie is more powerful than she let on, and she's been lying to you all this time about how much magic she still has."

"Thanks to her siphoning remnants of power from old pieces of enchanted jewelry." I puffed out a breath. "Just when I thought I'd found a new friend, she turned on me."

"I've been reading up on fractured familiar bonds. There's a long history of things turning nasty when a bond goes bad. It's because they're so personal and intense. Like a broken love affair," Sage said. "The familiars can get weird. Dangerously weird."

"That makes sense," I replied. "When I found her inside Iona's house, she was testing different magical objects and complaining because they didn't work."

"She's using them to give herself some abilities, but the power is fading," Sage said. "If magically infused items don't get a reboot, they stop working."

"And since Minnie was exposed to the hexed heart while Iona worked on it," I said, "she'll have become used to that intense level of power. She can't function without it, so she needs a new source."

"It sounds like Iona was a collector. She must have kept various objects that Minnie exploited," Sage said.

"Minnie lied about never going to Iona's house because she knew it would arouse suspicion," I said. "She must have been going back there every day and hunting through Iona's things to give herself a bit more power."

"I'm amazed there's anything of value left there," Sage said.

"Maybe potential looters were too afraid to go inside the house," I said. "Since the hexed heart murdered Iona, troublemakers would have been cautious of dark magic triggering and infecting them."

"And Iona had no living family, children, or partner, so the house has been stuck with no one to claim it or care for it," Sage said. "Minnie was free to sneak in and out whenever she liked."

"After the way Minnie's behaved, I'm making no more friends," I said. "They only betray me. They always do."

"Is that so?" Sage sat back. "When did I last betray you?"

"You steal my food," I said.

"That's not betrayal. That's a case of whoever gets there first is the winner. You need to stop being so down. Look on the positive. You survived your last encounter with Midnight."

"Barely! And that's a positive?"

"It's progress. Stop feeling so sorry for yourself. How will you track down Minnie?" Sage asked. "With a distorted bond muddying her thoughts, she'll be dangerous to handle on your own."

After a few seconds of grumbling, I realized there was no point in dwelling on my misery. I could only control this immediate moment. The past stayed where it was, and the future had yet to happen.

"Minnie must need to return regularly to Iona's house," I said. "If I lay traps there, I could capture her."

"What kind of traps are you talking about? You want to risk magic?"

"Yes. They'll need to be magical," I said.

"Then you'll need help," Sage said. "I can give you some pointers, but I can't offer much value from this distance."

I sighed. "Even though you do steal my food, I wish you were here."

"Me too. But there are others you could ask for help."

"Whiskers and Midnight?" I suggested tentatively.

"There you go. I knew we hadn't swapped personalities. You never give up, no matter the challenge facing you."

"I want to give up," I said. "Every bone aches. I'm covered in bruises. I'm always hungry. And I miss Zandra."

"And we all miss you, too. But let's focus on what you can change right now," Sage said. "No more moping. Gather your friends and lay those traps to catch that conniving cat once and for all."

I narrowed my gaze. "We really have swapped roles. Okay, let's go see if Midnight wants to be friendly or flay me."

# Chapter 18

"I'm still in shock. Minnie was always kooky, but I never figured her for a killer," Whiskers said, perched on top of a white marble mausoleum on the edge of the cemetery.

"She had me fooled too," I said. "I considered Minnie an ally. She was desperate to find out what happened to Iona. She seemed so genuine in her grief."

"Desperate to cover up the truth, more like." Midnight lounged on a pile of freshly turned earth.

He'd been pleasingly receptive to letting me into the cemetery, but only after Whiskers had pleaded my case. And he did a good job, but then he needed to, since he owed me a favor.

"We need to figure out how to bring Minnie down," I said.

"I'm not sure how I feel about killing Minnie," Whiskers said. "I mean, she's done a terrible thing, but—"

"I don't mean murder!" I said. "She's a killer, though. She must face justice."

"Minnie's been around a long time. She has more power than me," Whiskers said.

"She doesn't me," Midnight said. "But I'm still not sure I want to help. Or that Morticia would even allow it. We had a dozen new holes filled recently, and some of the newly dead are being giant jerks."

"Morticia doesn't have to know what you're doing," I said. "Surely you don't need to run everything past your witch."

"Morticia is much more than a witch," Whiskers cautioned. "Midnight and Morticia are tightly bonded. It's a special bond. Unique."

Midnight reached up and smacked him on the head with a paw. "Stop giving away my secrets. My bond with Morticia is not anyone's business but mine."

Whiskers ducked. "We're friends with Juno, so she needs to be in the know."

"The need-to-know is enough," Midnight said. "And she's only here because she doesn't have enough magic to do this herself. She wouldn't ask us otherwise."

"Untrue! I have a great group of friends who'd help me on missions when I lived in Crimson Cove," I said. "We brought down some of the worst criminals in the area as a team."

"Yeah, well, things aren't so great in Crimson Cove now," Midnight said.

My ears lifted. "What do you know?"

"Just rumors about magic going rogue, and the angels not figuring things out."

"No surprise there," Whiskers muttered. "I've almost forgotten what an angel looks like. We haven't had one in this village for a long time."

"I visited here with Finn not so long ago when we investigated another murder," I said.

"That doesn't count. We need a permanent Angel Force presence to keep things stable," Whiskers said.

"Never gonna happen," Midnight muttered. "They know this place is a lost cause. We're the lost cats. The outcast cats."

"Getting back to Crimson Cove," I said. "Tell me what's going on. That's where my witch lives. I need to know she's safe."

"I doubt she's safe," Midnight said. "But even if she's in peril, what can you do about it? You're trapped here, and you've got barely any power."

That was spectacularly unhelpful. "Tell me about Crimson Cove."

"Settle your hackles. There's nothing else to tell. Maybe it's just rumors," Midnight said.

That worrying news made me even more determined to get home as soon as possible, which meant capturing Minnie and getting answers from her.

"Will you help me trap Minnie?" I asked. "Once she's caught, she'll have to confess."

"She might," Midnight said. "And then again, she's got nothing to lose. Maybe she'll be happy with a life behind bars. At least she'd have shelter and regular meals."

I turned away from Midnight in disgust and focused on Whiskers. "Will you help? You owe me after almost getting me killed."

Whiskers winced. "That was a mistake. And I got you in here. I've repaid the favor."

"It'll take more than this to earn my forgiveness," I said. "And it didn't feel like a mistake when you herded me into a trap and tried to take me out."

"That was mainly the fake Roland's doing," Whiskers said. "I haven't put a paw wrong since then, have I?"

"I've barely seen you, so it's hard to know for sure," I said. "Some friend you are."

"Maybe... maybe I have been avoiding you," Whiskers said. "I feel guilty about what happened."

"Make it up to me now! Help me bring in Minnie for this crime, and we'll call it even."

"What magic will you use to trap her?" Midnight asked.

"Are you interested because you want to help or because you want to make snide comments about my suggestions?" I asked.

"Both. I'm open-minded."

I hissed at him. "I'll use a mixture of magical and non-magical traps. The kind used to catch wild animals. We use them sometimes at animal control."

Midnight narrowed his eyes. "You work for that forsaken place?"

"I used to. And its reputation is completely inaccurate," I said. "But let's focus on this mission. We can cast binding spells set with a trigger, so when Minnie crosses them, she's trapped and can't move. We'll also set a few cages and put wards around them, which means when she gets inside, she won't be able to get out. We'll lace the traps with tinned ham. She can't resist tinned ham."

"Ward alerts around the doors of Iona's old house would be a good move," Whiskers said.

"You're only using non-lethal means?" Midnight scoffed. "I forgot that you never met Iona, so you have no clue what power she wielded. That power is still in Minnie."

"Iona used her power for good," I said. "She treated people with emotional trauma. That magic can't be used for bad."

"Try telling that to the hexed heart," Midnight said. "That was allegedly forged to be used only for good, yet it killed someone as powerful as Iona."

We glared at each other. Midnight was being deliberately obtuse.

Whiskers cleared his throat. "I like the idea of a mix of magic. It covers all the bases. You've got the magic and the traditional. One of them will work."

"You always were too optimistic," Midnight said. "But I'm in."

"Are you sure you don't need your witch's permission?" I sniped.

"Watch it, or I'll turn you into a stone angel and sit you over the recently dead grindle beast." Midnight yawned. "And it'll be amusing when I see you fail."

"Don't get involved if you don't want to help."

Midnight lifted one shoulder. "I might throw in a spell or two just because I feel sorry for you."

"Ignore him." Whiskers said. "He's grumpy because Morticia has him doing the night shift."

"And part of the day shift." Midnight growled. "I've had barely any sleep. But it doesn't affect my abilities. I could capture Minnie with a paw tied behind my back, one eye closed, and neither of you helping."

I rolled my eyes and glanced at Whiskers, who shrugged in response.

"Let's get to work," I said. "We need to set the traps. The sooner I catch Minnie, the sooner I can figure out what to do with her."

"I still think annihilation is the best course of action," Midnight said. "But you're the boss on this one."

I paused. I often turned to obliteration when protecting my witch, but something had changed. A lot had changed, but maybe my thinking had altered, too. I had to hope it was for the better.

We left the cemetery and headed toward Iona's house. The streets were their usual gray, un-cozy, dismal selves, and the few people we saw soon scurried off, avoiding eye contact.

Along the way, we stopped, and Whiskers went into a store to order cages to be delivered to Iona's house that afternoon. With that matter settled, we made the final leg of the journey.

"Do we need to worry about protection wards?" Whiskers peered up at the neglected building.

"Nothing stopped me getting in when I followed Minnie inside," I said.

Midnight sauntered ahead. "Iona's wards will have faded into nothing. And it seems Minnie is too focused on getting her next magical hit to worry about anyone sneaking in."

After a quick check to ensure no one was watching us, we slipped into Iona's house, and settled into the least dusty room to get to work. We put trigger wards around the windows and doors, and containment nets over the entrances and exits. Whichever way Minnie came in, we'd catch her.

I used what little magic I had, sparking out a few spells, but Midnight dismissed my magic with a snooty paw wave and flooded the house with dozens of spells, one after the other, until the place shimmered with an eerie, chilly magic. It wasn't exactly dark magic, but grave magic had a gray tang to it. The sort that made you shiver the second you touched it.

An hour later, a gruff, red-faced man delivered the cages. We speedily set them up, doors open, spring-loaded, and some tempting ham treats waiting inside, which may have been borrowed from a nearby convenience store.

"Now all we have to do is wait," I said. "Let's get settled in."

"I'll search for snacks," Whiskers said. "I should have ordered in on our way over, but it's too late now."

Twenty minutes later, we were chewing on the fairly edible dried jerky Whiskers had found in the back of Iona's pantry. Midnight had found a tin of tuna but refused to share.

We waited three hours before the first sign of movement outside, just as dusk fell.

Midnight peered out through the window, growling softly. "It's just a honey badger. Stay out of their way. They're feisty."

"I met a nice one once," I said. "Angel Force accused him of murdering a vampire, but once I got to know him, he was great company."

"Did he snuff out the vamp?" Midnight asked.

"No, he was innocent."

Midnight arched his back and turned in a circle. "Are you sure Minnie did this?"

"Why did she lie to me about never coming here?" I asked. "Minnie said there were too many terrible memories, but she was sneaking over and testing the magical residue in Iona's personal things."

Midnight chewed on the end of his tail. "I heard a rumor that the hexed heart has an addictive quality."

I glanced at him. "You hear a lot of rumors."

"Because I keep my ears open and my mouth shut. Listen twice as much as you talk, and you learn a lot."

That was a fair point. "What did this rumor about the hexed heart reveal?"

"Some people got obsessed with it. Others, not so much. I suppose if you have an addictive personality, it would latch on and manipulate you."

"The hexed heart's magic wasn't supposed to be unpleasant," I said. "Iona would never have owned it if it harmed her clients."

"Maybe that was the idea," Midnight said. "But we all know Crispin's a giant jerk who wouldn't know what honest was if it jumped out of his toilet and bit him on the end of his—"

"Nose!" Whiskers said.

"Yeah, that's exactly what I was gonna say." Midnight smirked.

"Crispin got himself in trouble over another piece of jewelry a client commissioned him to make, didn't he?" I asked.

"So, you listen to rumors too," Midnight said.

"I read the case file. Angel Force knew about it, but nothing ever came of it."

"Crispin will make any kind of jewelry if he gets a big enough payment," Midnight said. "I don't trust that guy. If I had to pin this murder on anyone, I'd say it was him."

"But Angel Force never charged him," I said.

"Because they're cowards. They always have to gather one more piece of evidence before making a decision, or have one more committee meeting, and then vote. It's a lousy way to hand out justice."

"They hesitate before doing anything decisive," I said, "which is why I often have to step in. I see injustice occurring and fix it."

"You got in their way and made them your enemy, more like," Midnight said. "Otherwise, you wouldn't be stuck here."

I was about to protest, but shut my mouth. There was no point. I knew the truth, and I knew I was on the path to getting home.

"Hey! Shush. Something is moving outside," Whiskers whispered.

"It's probably that honey badger back again," Midnight said. "Maybe it smells our food."

Whiskers hopped onto a window ledge and peered out. He jumped back instantly, his eyes wide. "It's Minnie!"

"I knew she couldn't keep away for long," I said.

"A bonded familiar with no witch needs to get magic from somewhere," Midnight said. "There's no way she'd be able to keep going for this long without a source of power."

I nodded. Minnie was siphoning power to stay alive. I felt some sympathy for her situation, but I hated being lied to. Especially when that lie made her look guilty.

"Nobody move," I whispered. "Whichever way Minnie comes in, she'll be trapped, but we can't risk scaring her off."

We stayed still, listening for a trap or a ward being triggered.

"Minnie's being cautious," Midnight whispered.

"Because she knows I'm on to her," I replied.

There was a fizzle of magic, followed by a small squeak and then scrabbling noises close to the back door.

"We've got her. Let's go!" I bounded into the kitchen to find Minnie slicing through a containment net with vicious claws. She was free within seconds.

"She's making a run for it!" Whiskers yelled.

Midnight growled, leaping into the hall ahead of me. "I told you your nets were weak."

"Less sass, and more stopping her," I snapped, veering left as Minnie bolted toward a bedroom.

She hurled a burst of raw magic at Whiskers, who ducked just in time. The fireball scorched the wallpaper and set an old velvet curtain smoldering.

Whiskers hissed, flinging a containment charm that fizzled midair. "She's warded with protection spells."

Minnie turned and flicked her tail. A shelf burst open, showering me with dried herbs and old teacups. One cracked against my head. I staggered but kept going.

I scrabbled up a tiny spell, a binding loop made of borrowed magic. It sparked, dim and shaky, but I hurled it anyway. It caught Minnie's hind leg for half a second, just long enough for Whiskers to fire another containment spell.

The magic struck true this time.

Minnie stumbled, slowed, snarled, then spun in a desperate circle. "Let me go. You don't understand. I need it!"

Midnight appeared behind her. He muttered something under his breath. A dark, coiling net of energy formed around Minnie's shoulders, then dropped like a weighted net.

She hit the floor and didn't get up. "I didn't mean to hide things. I just wanted... I needed more."

I was too exhausted and furious to answer. I looked down at Minnie, tangled in a web of spells and remorse. "You're under arrest for Iona's murder."

# Chapter 19

"This place doesn't change much," Midnight said, glancing around the library with a long sigh, deeply unimpressed as he helped haul open a small closet.

"It's home for now," I replied. "It has everything I need."

"Ghosts. Dust. And boring books?"

"Safety. Warmth. And knowledge."

Midnight grunted.

"Did you get her?" Sage's voice came out of the snow globe.

Midnight spun around and hissed. "Who's that? I thought you lived here on your own?"

"It's my friend Sage," I said. "She's been helping with the investigations."

Midnight spied the globe. He glared at Sage for a second before turning back to the closet. "You really won't reconsider your stance on annihilation? Minnie has guilt scrawled all over her scrawny form. We'd be doing the angels a favor."

"I prefer obliteration when it comes to my true enemies," I said, "but I need Minnie to talk before sentencing is carried out."

"I've already talked!" Minnie said with a low whimper, still bound by magic so she couldn't escape. "I didn't do it. I know I lied to you, and I'm sorry for that, but I had my reasons. Good reasons. Why won't you listen to the truth?"

"I know what that reason is," I said, "but you still have questions to answer and a confession to make."

"Make the containment in this closet as strong as possible," Midnight said as he peered in at the old cleaning supplies and boxes. "She's still got power. Minnie is sneaky."

"I didn't get any power tonight," Minnie said. "And I need some. I must have some. I get sick if I don't have it."

"You sound just like Lavender," I said. "Whiskers, will you do the honors with the containment magic?"

He stretched out his front legs and shook his fur before throwing out several spells that covered the closet, blocking any chance of escape.

"Do you want us to stay? I can get out the paw screws if she doesn't cooperate?" Midnight asked.

"Thanks, but I've got it from here," I said.

"You know where we are if you need anyone to rough her up." Midnight turned and walked away. Whiskers shrugged, then followed him.

"Did any of your new friends misbehave?" Sage asked.

"It was touch and go whether Midnight would get his paws involved, but he came through in the end," I said.

"And Minnie fell into your trap," Sage said. "Good. Now get her to confess."

"I've been trying on our way here," I said. "She's refusing to cooperate."

"I can't confess to something I didn't do," Minnie said from inside the closet. "I really am sorry for deceiving you. I like you. Both of you."

"Minnie, the evidence is stacked against you," I said. "You were with Iona when she was killed."

"And as I've already explained, the magic used to kill her messed with my memory too. That night is a horrible, blurry nothing!"

"You lied about never going back to Iona's house," I said. "After I read your statement from Angel Force, I followed you and saw you go inside. You went inside the house and siphoned magic."

Minnie hesitated, her gaze downcast. "I... yes. Maybe I did do that."

"There's no maybe about it. I saw you," I said. "I understand. You need power to keep going, but why lie about that? It's not shameful. I'd expect you to do it so you could stay alive."

"You lied. You had the opportunity, and you had a motive," Sage said.

"What's my motive?" Minnie asked.

"Your familiar bond fractured because Iona became obsessed with the hexed heart. You were jealous and lashed out. Or maybe you wanted the hexed heart's power all to yourself," Sage said.

"Or you felt abandoned," I replied. "It can be frustrating when your witch gets obsessed with something other than you."

"None of that is true." Minnie trembled. "I loved Iona. I'd never hurt her. My role was to protect her."

"Yet you didn't, when she needed you the most," Sage said. "Because there was no one to protect her from other than you."

"It wasn't me!"

I sighed. "You were at the crime scene. You have no alibi. You have motive and opportunity, and when I tried to talk to you, you ran from me."

"Because I panicked. I was worried you'd find out the truth about me."

"What truth would that be?" I asked.

Minnie looked away, her whiskers trembling. "You should question Crispin again. I'm sure he's behind what happened to Iona."

"Don't point the paw at someone else. That won't distract us," I said.

"He has to be involved," Minnie said. "Talk to him again. He's the guilty one. He made that horrible hexed heart. And it's not the only unstable magical artifact he's created."

Midnight had also pointed at Crispin, but if Minnie was our killer, then it didn't matter what dubious activities Crispin got up to. Well, it did, but I'd deal with that another time.

"Please just dig deeper into Crispin," Minnie said. "I know he killed Iona."

I huffed out a breath. "Sage, get Finn to look into Crispin's background in more detail. It's possible he's been dabbling in some dark stuff. Getting people injured."

"I can if I want to waste my time," Sage said. "Have you changed your mind about Minnie being the killer?"

"No. I still think she's guilty," I said. "But if Crispin is making dangerous artifacts, then Angel Force needs to know, so they can stop him."

"I'll ask." Sage's gaze flicked over my head. "Check on Minnie. She doesn't look so good."

I turned back to find Minnie hunched on the closet floor, shaking. "What's wrong with you?"

"I'm terrified you'll send me away for murdering my witch when I didn't do it."

I inched closer, careful not to breach the wards that kept her trapped inside the closet. "It's the hexed heart, isn't it? You're suffering from magic withdrawal."

Minnie raised a shaking paw and attempted to wash one ear. "No."

"If I asked you to walk in a straight line, could you?"

"I... maybe I need help. The heart was so powerful that it took both of us by surprise."

"You must have known its history," I said. "Crispin wasn't honest about how powerful the brooch was, but Iona must have sensed its potential."

"Even Iona was shocked by the magic coming out of it. She said it would revolutionize our practice, and she'd be able to help hundreds more people. I felt it too. The raw power lurking in that brooch."

"And it was too much of a temptation," I said. "You started siphoning off that magic, then realized you couldn't let go. Is that why you killed Iona? She discovered you'd become addicted to the magical properties and cut you off?"

"Iona never knew I'd grown so fond of the magic."

"Fond?" Sage snorted. "You're an addict! And addicts do terrible things when they can't get their next fix or someone tries to help them when they're not ready."

Minnie gulped. "I'll admit I lost control around the hexed heart. I used to sneak tiny sips of its power. For a time, it was enough to keep me going."

"But not for long. And looking at you now, you're desperate to find a replacement." I glanced at where the cold case file sat on the desk. "Is that why you came here? Because I reopened the cold case? There's a brooch in the box file. Did you sense it?"

"I... I didn't make friends with you because of that," Minnie said.

"I smell a big fat lie," Sage said. "You were using Juno."

"I like Juno! I like both of you. But when you opened that case file, it broke the seal that contained the magic," Minnie said. "I felt the power call to me."

"And you had to be near it," I said. "You wanted its power, just like you wanted it when Iona was alive, yet she stood in your way."

"I figured that brooch was inert. It still has magic in it?" Sage asked.

Minnie shook even more. "It'll always have a hold on me. The hexed heart took over. It controlled us. We both misused it. Neither of us spoke about it because we were ashamed. And I thought that over time, we'd get used to the extra magic it gave us, but it never stabilized."

"So, you kept going back for more and more," I said. "What went wrong?"

"Not murder! Even though I know you think I killed Iona," Minnie said. "But there was a complication."

"What was the complication?" Sage asked.

Minnie gulped again. "I... I bonded to the hexed heart. I'm not sure how it happened, but one day I accessed its magic, and it flooded through me. It changed me. I felt my abilities evolve, and suddenly my bond with Iona weakened. It was still there, but it had altered. I felt more loyalty to the hexed heart than to my witch. It was shameful."

"And its power told you to get rid of Iona because she was a liability?" I asked.

"Never! The hexed heart has kindness at its core. At least, it did until something went wrong with the magic. It was Crispin, I'm telling you. He tampered with it. He was always jealous of Iona. He wanted to work with her, but she would have nothing to do with him. She belittled him." Minnie was panting, her fur soaked with sweat.

"You went to Iona's house this evening to get more magic, didn't you?" I asked. "What will happen if you don't get it?"

"I've only ever gone a day or so without recharging," Minnie said. "The way I'm feeling, I won't make it through the night."

I glanced at Sage. "Is there anything I can do for her? She's obviously having a magical detox."

"Give me a minute to check the books," Sage said and disappeared from view.

I stood in front of Minnie. "How long were you misusing the warped magic?"

"We'd been accessing the power within the hexed heart for months," Minnie said. "It felt so good. Yes, it was strong, and I admit I felt compelled to use more and more of it, but there was no malevolence within that magic. It just wanted me to be the very best version of myself."

"Perhaps the magic decided Iona wasn't good enough for you. It forced you to tamper with the energy. When Iona attempted to access it, it killed her."

"That's not what happened," Minnie said. "Iona was happy that evening. Sure, she'd fought with Lavender, but she was confident in her ability to help people and control the hexed heart. She saw so much potential in it. We both did."

Minnie's story was compelling, but there was too much stacked against her. She had to be guilty.

"I've got something," Sage said. "Go grab mugwort, valerian, lemon balm oil, and some of those ground mouse bones you found the other week. Mix them into a tincture and get Minnie to drink it. It'll speed her through the detox symptoms. She'll feel rough for a few hours but will be better in the morning."

"Will you take the tincture if I make it for you?" I asked Minnie.

"I'll take it. But without getting a magic boost, I don't have long left."

"Then confess," I said. "Do the right thing for your witch. Your bond was fractured, but you owe her that much."

"I can't confess to something I didn't do," Minnie said. "And I'm begging you, speak to Crispin again. I know it was him."

"We'll come back to this in the morning," I said. Minnie was stumbling over her words and shaking so badly she really looked like she wouldn't survive the night. "I'll make your tincture. Then you rest."

"And I'll look into Crispin, even though I think it's a waste of time," Sage said.

I nodded. It made sense to cover all the bases, even though from where I stood, I looked straight at Iona's killer.

# Chapter 20

I rolled out of my makeshift bed of scrunchy newspaper, cushioned by an old curtain I'd found discarded in one corner. I did a big stretch and headed to the closet.

It had been a restless night. Minnie struggled with her magical detox, and although the tincture Sage had instructed me to make took the edge off, Minnie had gone through a nasty detox before she felt even marginally better.

I peeked in at her through the protective wards. She was in a deep sleep, her chest rising slowly, although her paws twitched occasionally, suggesting she was dreaming.

I glanced up at the silent snow globe. Sage would still be slumbering, no doubt tucked against Vorana's side, warm, cozy, and happy with her witch.

That was where I wanted to be. Solving this crime would get me home. I had to hope. There had to be a way back to Crimson Cove and Zandra.

A quick kibble breakfast and a slurp of water, and I was ready to tie up the loose ends in this case. All I needed was Minnie's confession, and then Sage would do the rest, letting Angel Force know we'd found Iona's killer. They could put this cold case in the solved pile, where it deserved to be, and I'd get a gold star.

I went back and peeked in at Minnie. Her eyes were open, and she blinked at me once.

"Greetings!" I said. "I'm glad to see you got some sleep."

She didn't lift her head, simply lay flat on her belly, looking forlorn. "I feel awful. Please let me out. I know how I can make myself feel better."

"This is short-term pain for long-term gain," I said. "If you keep patching up the problem by borrowing magic, you'll prolong the agony."

"Why do you care?" Minnie asked. "It's not as if we're friends."

"And I'm sorry for that," I replied. "I liked you, and I wanted to help you solve what happened to your witch, yet you deceived me and lied to me. You knew what happened all along."

Minnie turned her head away from the door. "You can keep me in here forever, and I'll never confess."

The snow globe brightening caught my eye, and I left Minnie to her moroseness and hopped onto the desk to see Sage's face come into view.

"You have scrambled egg on your whiskers," I said by way of greeting.

Sage pawed the egg out of her whiskers and ate it off her pad. "I thought you'd want to know the news about Crispin as soon as possible."

"What did Finn find out?" I settled on the desk.

"Crispin Vance is a sleazy, tricky, untrustworthy guy," Sage said. "It took Finn some digging, and he had to ask his shadier contacts before he got the real lowdown on Crispin. The guy has been peddling his services to whoever pays him enough. He doesn't care what it's for or who it could hurt."

I glanced back at Minnie. "That's what our prisoner said."

"I don't know if it means he's your killer," Sage said. "But he's dodgy. Finn spoke to a couple of demons in the Crypt witch prison who've used his services. They paid him handsomely to create jewelry with negative enchantments. They were gifts for their enemies. One blew up, and the other sent the magic user insane."

I leaned closer to the snow globe and lowered my voice. "Do you think Minnie's telling the truth? Even with all the evidence against her?"

"She's our killer all right," Sage said. "But it's worth confronting Crispin. I reckon he knew what he was doing with the hexed heart. Maybe Minnie got him to manipulate the magic, so when Iona used it, it went boom."

"Which means he's an accomplice to murder," I said. "Angel Force can arrest him and stop him from peddling his dubious services to anyone else and causing more harm."

"It's worth a conversation with him to see if he's willing to make a deal," Sage said.

"Crispin may crack now we have Minnie in custody," I replied. "He could be afraid she'll reveal the truth, hoping to get a plea deal."

"And they end up implicating each other," Sage said. "Two bad apples scooped out of the barrel and squished before they can do any more damage."

"Angel Force will have to visit Badger's Haze and arrest him. Tell Finn to make the arrangements."

"He's already put in a request to Cythera. She's thinking about it," Sage said. "Don't hold your breath, though. Cythera's been in a foul mood for days."

"Is there an external audit scheduled? Or a visit from those pesky higher angels?" I asked. "Those events always send Cythera into a tailspin of grumpiness."

Sage snort-laughed. "I wish it were only that."

Worry trickled through me. "Midnight mentioned problems with Crimson Cove's magic. Is it that? Should I be worried?"

"We've got a handle on things," Sage said.

"What does that mean?"

"It means you focus on solving this mystery. We're not powerless around here. Especially not since I got a jolt of your magic."

That did little to settle my unease. "I'd come back and help if I could."

"I know. Now go question that shady jewelry maker and see what he has to say for himself," Sage said. "I can see Minnie from here, so I'll watch her."

I checked on Minnie, but she'd turned away from the door and was pretending to sleep.

After a quick goodbye to Sage, I headed out into the weak morning sunlight, an unnatural fog lingering over the streets as I marched along, heading for Crispin's store.

I had to knock several times before he opened the door.

He looked down at me and frowned. "I hope you're not here to fake buy again?"

"I need to ask a few more questions," I said. "I've found Iona's killer."

Crispin's eyebrows shot up. Was that relief I saw on his face?

He nudged the door open and gestured me inside. "That's great news. Who did it?"

"Her familiar. Minnie," I said.

"Huh. Well, I suppose that makes sense."

"Why do you say that?" I followed Crispin to the counter.

He stood behind it, a mug of coffee on top. "I always considered Minnie quirky. She had these funny little habits. She had to have her water bowls in specific places, and she liked to sleep in a shoebox that was too small for her."

"That's typical cat behavior," I said. "Nothing strange about that."

Crispin glanced at me. "If you say so. And she was always watching Iona."

"That's a familiar's job," I said. "We keep our magic users safe."

"It was intense watching," Crispin said. "And she'd be interested in any magic Iona cast. She'd ask questions about it."

"Again, not odd," I replied. "I'm always interested in what my witch does with her magic."

Crispin grunted. "Well, anyway, I always thought Minnie was strange, so hearing she actually killed Iona is no shock."

"Minnie must have known how to manipulate the hexed heart for it to malfunction and kill Iona," I said.

He grimaced. "I still hate that name for it. But you're right, she would. And she'd have known exactly what to do. Like I said, Minnie was always watching."

"Do you consider her powerful enough to manipulate an enchanted piece of jewelry you crafted?"

"Iona was powerful, so I assume Minnie is just as strong," Crispin said. "It wouldn't have been easy for her to manipulate the magic, but not impossible."

"If she'd paid you enough, would you have done it for her?" I asked.

Crispin lowered his mug slowly, and his eyes narrowed. "Why would I do that?"

"For the reason I just stated. You have no quibbles about taking money to create pieces of enchanted jewelry that clients demand. It doesn't matter to you if the enchantments are legal."

"That's an outrage! I run a legitimate business," Crispin said.

"Not according to two demons serving sentences in the Crypt witch prison."

"I know nothing about that," Crispin said. "And you should never trust a demon's words. They lie to get what they want or simply to cause problems. It's in their nature."

"These demons had no reason to lie," I said.

"Then they lied for the fun of it," Crispin said.

"Or they're telling the truth, and you're making illegal pieces of enchanted jewelry, knowing the buyer's intention is impure," I said. "You don't care what happens to the person wearing it so long as you get paid enough."

Crispin thumped down his mug and crossed his arms over his chest. "I had nothing to do with what happened to Iona. You have your killer. If Minnie is proving a tough cat to crack, that's your concern. Not mine."

"We may not be able to implicate you in what happened to Iona," I said, "but Angel Force will be visiting. They'll want to know how shady your business practices are and decide if you can continue operating."

"Don't get Angel Force meddling. My business has nothing to do with them," Crispin said. "Besides, they aren't interested in what goes on in Badger's Haze."

"Illegally created hexed pieces of jewelry are most definitely their concern," I said.

"They'll never waste their time coming here," Crispin replied. "I've been running this business for years, and I've not had so much as a sniff of an angel nearby. They're scared to visit this lawless place. So they should be."

"Don't be surprised if they make an exception just for you," I said. "Especially if you were involved in Iona's murder."

Crispin tutted. "Get a confession from Minnie and leave me alone."

"And if I don't?"

Crispin's nostrils flared. "You'll find yourself with your own piece of hexed jewelry." He marched to the door and snatched it open.

I glared at him for a few seconds before stepping outside. The door slammed, and I was alone with only my irritation. But only for a few seconds.

Whiskers and Midnight marched toward me.

"Greetings!" I said.

"Sage said you needed us," Whiskers said.

If I had eyebrows, they'd have shot up. "You're in contact with Sage?"

"Of course. Well, we've never met in person, but she sent us a message." Whiskers had a gleeful expression on his face.

I glanced at Midnight. He was smirking. "Unless it's urgent, I'm busy. I've just been speaking to Crispin about his dodgy business practices."

"That can wait." Midnight nudged me with his nose. "You have an appointment at the tattoo parlor."

# Chapter 21

I choked out a laugh. "That was Sage's urgent message?"

"She said you'd back out if we don't go with you to get it done. Move. You don't want to be late." Midnight headbutted me in the side.

"I have to get Minnie's murder confession!" I protested. "Which means I have no time to get a foolish tattoo."

"You have plenty of time." Midnight growled at me. "Sage said Minnie is sleeping, and she's still refusing to confess. Give her time to stew and think about what she's done. While she's pondering her next move, you're getting ink."

"How do you even know about this?" I backed away.

"Sage! You lost the deal," Whiskers said. "You have to go through with it. It's the noble thing to do."

"I wish I'd never said anything about a tattoo," I grumbled.

"They don't hurt," Midnight said. "Much."

"It probably will," Whiskers said. "It depends on where you have it done."

I groaned, but allowed them to nudge me toward the small, rather run-down tattoo parlor with black and white paint flaking on the outside of the building. I took a moment to peer through the slightly grubby window at all the tattoos on display.

"I'm only getting something tiny," I said.

"You should go for a full head tattoo," Midnight said. "Make a bold statement."

"I'm doing nothing that involves any fur being shaved off," I retorted. "Can we not postpone this until another day?"

"Stop stalling. Get inside." Midnight roughly headbutted me again. "Don't make me bite you."

"Shouldn't you be guarding graves or chasing skeletons?" I grumbled.

"Morticia's in a bad mood, so I escaped," Midnight said.

"I got him out," Whiskers said. "I was on my way to see you to bring you here when I heard Morticia screeching. I figured Midnight needed a laugh... I mean, a break."

I sighed heavily, then shuffled inside the tattoo parlor. Although the outside was bleak, the reception area was sparklingly clean.

A petite female elf with multi-colored tattoos running up the side of her neck and finishing behind her ear smiled when we entered.

"You must be Juno," she said to me. "You're my first familiar. I'm so excited to give you some ink."

"Greetings. I wish I could say the same." I looked around. It was immaculately clean, with a white-tiled floor that gleamed. Quiet classical rock played in the background. It wasn't what I'd expected.

"Is this your first time getting ink?" the tattoo artist asked.

"Yes," I said, "and I'm hoping it'll be my last."

"You'll get a taste for it once you've had your first." She crouched and held out a hand. "Lola."

I lifted my paw so we could shake. "Will you numb the area? I don't want to feel a thing."

"You have a high pain threshold," Midnight said. "At least you should. Don't be a wimp."

"I'm being practical," I said.

"I can put numbing gel over the area I ink," Lola said. "Now, what are you thinking? Big, small, colored, black? The choice is yours. I can do different styles, from cartoon to photorealistic."

"Nothing complex or time-consuming," I said. "Just something small on one toe bean."

"That's a coward's choice," Midnight said. "Juno is getting her head shaved, and you're doing the entire skull."

"No, I'm not," I replied. "And since you're so obsessed with head tattoos, why don't you get in line for ink?"

Midnight smirked. "You have no idea what's under this fur."

Lola chuckled and stood up. "Take your time looking around. The small tattoos are on the left wall, and as you work your way along, they get more elaborate. I'll be out back getting ready. Just shout when you've found something."

I thanked her and then trudged behind Whiskers and Midnight, who were already studying the smaller tattoos. Although I didn't want a tattoo, there were some lovely designs. Swirls. Mini mandalas. Spirals. Stars. Hearts.

"I suppose I could get a tiny cat on my paw," I said.

"Of yourself? Arrogant much?" Midnight said. "I like this full tattoo sleeve of a ghost eating a demon."

"I'm getting nothing like that!" I said. "Perhaps a star."

"Because you are one." Midnight sneered at me.

"What about a small witch's cauldron?" Whiskers asked. "That would be cute. Or a mini broomstick."

We worked our way along the wall, and I spent a few moments looking at attractive tattoos inked on the backs of hands with swirls and colors. There were also beautiful tattoos of familiars that looked startlingly realistic.

I stopped by a wrist tattoo. It looked familiar. "I've seen this before."

"Dr. Greaves has that tattoo," Whiskers said. "She had it done years ago."

"Of course! When she helped me out of the swamp pond, I saw it on her wrist," I said.

"Why were you in there?" Midnight asked.

"Long story." I gently sniffed my fur, convinced the stench of that gross encounter still lingered.

"Dr. Greaves never struck me as the type to get a tattoo," Midnight said. "Still, people are full of surprises. Usually ones that disappoint."

I studied the tattoo for a second. It was beautiful, done in multiple colors with twirls and swirls across the skin.

"Have you made your mind up?" Lola came out of the back room, wearing a pair of gloves and holding a tattoo gun.

"I'll go for a small black star on my left paw. On one toe bean," I said.

"Excellent choice," Lola said. "If you hop on the counter, I'll get the ink prepped, and then we'll get to work."

"Don't forget to numb my paw," I said. "Give me double the dose."

"I won't forget." She smiled at me. "What do you think of the designs? They're all my work."

"They're incredible," I said. "I was admiring the one you did for Dr. Greaves."

"That was a long time ago." Lola glanced at the wall. "I had to be careful with that one because of the scar tissue. That was why she had it done."

"Oh, I didn't even notice the scar because of your beautiful art," I said.

"Yeah. She had a real mess on her wrist. It must have been sore, but Dr. Greaves insisted she wanted the tattoo as soon as possible. Some people are funny about scars, aren't they? Worried about what others will think."

"The swirls are unusual." I looked over at the wall. "Did Dr. Greaves design the piece herself?"

"No! That's the interesting thing." Lola dabbed a cool liquid onto my paw. "That design is in the shape of the scar. She asked me to ink the whole scar, following the contours so it would be hidden. The only way you'd know about the scar tissue now was if you stroked a paw over the skin."

I looked back at the picture and tilted my head.

"Don't be thinking up excuses not to get your tattoo," Midnight said. "We're staying here until the ink is done and wrapped."

I gasped and jumped off the table.

"Hey! Don't say you've changed your mind," Lola said. "It'll take ten minutes. I'll be gentle. You already have the first dot."

"Get back on that table!" Midnight snarled. "You're not leaving here until you've had your tattoo."

"There's no time for any ink," I said. "I've just discovered Minnie isn't the killer."

# Chapter 22

"I have an apology to make," I muttered to Sage as I crouched close to the snow globe.

"It seems you do," she said. "And I can't believe you actually went through with getting a tattoo. I was only teasing when I sent Midnight and Whiskers after you."

"I don't believe that for a second." I turned over my paw, where Lola had added a single dot of black ink before my startling revelation stopped the torture. "It's a start. Perhaps I'll get it finished once this case is over."

"Are you planning on staying in Badger's Haze, then?" Sage asked.

I puffed out a breath. "That's very much up to Angel Force."

"Iona was an influential figure," Sage said. "You solving her murder should count for something."

"It needs to count for everything if I'm to get back to Crimson Cove," I said. "Right. I need to get my apology over with and then confront our actual killer."

I hopped off the desk and headed to the closet, where the door stood open but the wards still shimmered, keeping Minnie trapped.

"How are you feeling?" I asked.

She didn't look at me, her eyes remaining shut. "Washed out. Tired. Heartsick. Why don't you get this over and done with? There's no point in keeping me here. You've made your mind up about my guilt, even though I told you a dozen different ways I didn't do it."

"I... I believe you," I said. "And I'm sorry for keeping you trapped here."

That caught Minnie's attention, and she lifted her head and opened her eyes. "Are you saying you think I'm innocent?"

I nodded. "New evidence has come to light."

"What evidence?" Minnie scrambled to her paws, staggering slightly as she hurried toward me.

"If you promise to behave, you can come with me while I reveal the killer," I said. "But you mustn't attack."

"Tell me their name," Minnie growled. "I'll destroy them."

"You'll stay behind those wards if you keep talking like that," I said.

"It was Crispin, wasn't it?" Minnie said. "I never trusted him. He's so false and smarmy."

"Crispin will get what's coming to him because of his shady business practices," I replied. "But he's innocent of murder."

"Then who did it?" Minnie asked.

"Give me your word you'll behave, and you'll soon find out," I said.

She wrinkled her nose and stamped her paws. "I won't kill them, but I may box them about the ears a few times. Maybe slash an arm."

"I'll allow that. Stand back." I focused on drawing down the wards. It took all my effort, but Minnie was finally released.

She stepped through the open doorway. "I can't believe you really solved it. After all these years, I thought I'd never find out what happened to Iona."

"I have to thank my new friends for forcing me into a tattoo parlor," I said. "That's where the answer was."

"Tattoos? I'm lost," Minnie said. "What do tattoos have to do with anything?"

"You'll find out. Follow me." I glanced at the snow globe. "Keep an eye on things here, Sage. I'll be back soon to update you."

"Take the recording spell I gave you!" she called out.

"I've already got it on me." Sage had gifted me a spell that recorded my movements in Badger's Haze when confronting a killer. It provided crucial evidence, so Angel Force had a record of all the good I did.

"Do you want me to alert Finn about what you're doing?" Sage asked around a mouthful of food.

I nodded. "He's one of the few angels brave enough to come here, and we need someone to apprehend our criminal."

"Hopefully, Cythera will have authorized his trip by now," Sage said. "That'll allow Angel Force to lower the barrier for a second to allow him through."

I drew in a breath. It could be my chance to get out of here. If I could sneak through when the barrier lowered to allow Finn in...

I sighed and shook my head. This case needed solving, and although I desperately wanted to get out and back to Zandra, I had to see this through to the end. Even if it meant I lost my chance of freedom. And if I escaped, the angels would drag me back and probably punish me even more.

"Good luck," Sage hollered.

I left the library with Minnie beside me, the chill making me fluff my fur.

Minnie hurried along, her nose twitching as she looked around. "Where are we going?"

"To see Dr. Thelma Greaves," I said.

"Do you need to look at the autopsy information again?" Minnie asked. "There wasn't much she could do after Iona turned to ash."

I adjusted the small backpack I wore into a more comfortable position, the heavy weight of the object inside painful against my shoulder blades. "She'll want to know what I've learned."

"She is smart. Did she tell you something about tattoos?"

"Just wait."

We walked in silence for a few minutes.

"What will you do once this has been resolved?" I asked. "There'll be no reason for you to stay in Badger's Haze."

Minnie huffed out a breath. "I... I don't know. I stayed alive because I had to find out what happened to Iona. But then I lost my way. That dumb hexed heart ruined us."

"The magic in the hexed heart was once pure," I said. "It got corrupted when our killer messed with it. That's where things went wrong. Iona didn't realize what power she wielded, and you got sucked into the mess too and became addicted to the magic."

"It did change." There was a wistful tint in Minnie's tone. "I thought about it after you locked me in the closet. The brooch channeled pure magic perfectly. Iona was so excited about its potential. But then one day, it felt different. It was just before Iona died. I should have realized something was wrong, but I was beguiled by it and didn't want to admit something had shifted."

"And I take it Iona was just as reluctant to admit the powerful magic had you both bespelled?" I asked.

"We didn't talk about it, but we were obsessed. We neglected each other in favor of that magic. I feel terrible. I should have been a better familiar."

"That must have been when it was tampered with," I said. "Perhaps it was a slow-release form of dark magic that slowly infiltrated both of you, and then it destabilized, killing Iona. It could just as easily have been you who died that night."

"Don't tell me I got lucky," Minnie said.

"There's nothing lucky about losing your bonded witch. It's a terrible thing. The worst thing that can happen," I said. "You grieve for as long as you need to. It's been a long time since Iona died, but that doesn't mean the grief becomes less sharp."

"It feels like I have a dagger in my heart." Minnie softly howled. "Sometimes, I just want to yank it out and give up. Other times, it hurts less. Will the pain ever end?"

"It will mellow over time, especially now you've got a resolution."

"Not yet, I haven't," Minnie said. "You still haven't told me who did it."

I stopped. "Here we are."

We entered a small building containing the morgue and hunted for a few moments until we discovered Dr. Greaves in a back room, looking over paperwork. She glanced up when she heard us at the door.

"Juno and... is that Minnie?"

"Surprise! I'm not dead." Minnie shuffled from paw to paw and ducked her head.

"I'm happy to see that. This really is a surprise. Was I expecting you?" Dr. Greaves glanced at an open paper diary.

"We've had a development in the investigation into what happened to Iona," I said. "I thought you'd be interested."

"Of course. Come in." She gestured to the two chairs on the opposite side of the desk.

We hopped into them, Minnie sliding me a curious look but making no comment.

Dr. Greaves gestured for me to continue.

"We looked into all the suspects and witnesses Angel Force initially interviewed," I said.

"That was sensible," Dr. Greaves said. "Did you uncover information the angels missed?"

"There were several people who could easily have done it," I said. "Not everyone had an alibi. Crispin Vance, for example."

"I wondered about him," Dr. Greaves said. "He's a curious type. And I'm not entirely sure his business is legitimate."

"It definitely isn't," I said. "He's manufacturing jewelry and enchanted artifacts for ridiculous sums of money, not caring that the magic will do harm."

"Oh! That's highly illegal," Dr. Greaves said. "Did Iona find out and threaten to reveal his secret?"

"She may have, but that's not the reason she was murdered," I said. "Even so, Crispin will soon be visited by the authorities to answer for his crimes."

"I'm glad to hear it," she said. "I'm intrigued, though. What did you learn about Iona's killer?"

"That they're sneaky and hiding in plain sight," I said. "They use their expertise to charm and beguile so no one suspects them."

"That's fascinating. I was about to say it could have been Hester Gull, but then you said the word 'charmed,' and realized that would be impossible." Dr. Greaves laughed lightly.

"Hester is unique," I said. "I understand she's not popular with many people because of her constant blackmailing and secret stealing."

"Yes, I've heard those rumors," Dr. Greaves said.

"Has she ever attempted to blackmail you?" I asked.

"Stars above! Of course not. I have nothing to hide."

I cocked my head. "Nothing?"

"Absolutely not." Dr. Greaves settled herself in her chair. "What did Hester have on Iona?"

"Not a thing. Hester had no dirt on Iona, so there was no motive for Hester to kill her."

"That is surprising. I'd overheard Iona belittle Hester's abilities more than once," Dr. Greaves said. "She used to laugh about her being able to whisper to birds, and what an irrelevant skill it was."

"Hester's magic is extraordinary," I said. "Being able to control such powerful familiars is no small feat. If that's what Iona said, then she was wrong to do so."

Minnie ducked her head. "Iona could be a little judgy."

Dr. Greaves's mouth tightened. "If it wasn't Crispin, and it wasn't Hester, then who? I remember Lavender was of interest to Angel Force because she discovered Iona's body."

"Lavender's eccentric ways raised questions," I said. "But Lavender is enamored with certain illegal magical substances. She was collecting those substances on the night of Iona's death. Hester's ravens saw her passed out after enjoying herself too much."

"Oh! Well, I've noticed her strange behavior," Dr. Greaves said. "Some people don't know their own limits."

"Or they don't think rules and limits apply to them."

Dr. Greaves hesitated, then her eyes brightened. "Delphine! It must be her. But she's too obvious. She despised Iona. The arguments they had turned the air blue. Do you remember, Minnie? All the screaming and yelling."

Minnie nodded slowly. "Delphine has a temper."

"There we have it!" Dr. Greaves slapped a hand on the desk. "Why didn't Angel Force figure this out? Even I considered Delphine the main suspect when it all happened."

"Because Delphine was asleep on top of her dead lover's grave on the night of the murder," I said.

"Goodness! Juno, few people startle me, but you are one of them." Dr. Greaves lowered her eyes for a second. "I did wonder, and please don't take offense at this, Minnie, but your relationship with Iona was complicated."

"Our bond was perfect!" Minnie's fur bristled. "At least it was until the hexed heart corrupted it. Or should I say, someone corrupted it."

"It is a terrible business when a magic user tries to control a power that is beyond them," Dr. Greaves said. "I've dealt with more than one autopsy where someone overstretched with a spell, and their death was the result."

"Iona could control the hexed heart, but only when it hadn't been tampered with," I said.

"It was tampered with?" Dr. Greaves asked. "By whom?"

"You know the answer to that," I replied.

"If I did, I'd have informed Angel Force when this all happened." Dr. Greaves stood from her seat. "And as interesting as this conversation is, I don't see that you've made any progress in finding out what happened to Iona."

"Could I see your tattoo?" I asked.

She glanced at her wrist. "Why do you want to do that?"

"It's hiding a scar, isn't it?"

Her eyes widened a fraction. "What business is that of yours?"

"I went to get a tattoo today, and I saw a picture of yours on the wall. Lola was obliging enough to tell me the story about why you got one."

"Lola talks too much," Dr. Greaves muttered. She tugged her sleeve over her wrist. "It's not an interesting story. I had a scar and decided to conceal it with something prettier."

"So soon after the injury happened?" I asked. "That must have been incredibly painful."

"The numbing magic worked fine. Now, if you don't mind, I have lots of work to do."

"I do mind," I said. "And I insist you show me your tattoo."

"And I insist you leave my office and stop wasting my time." Dr. Greaves narrowed her gaze.

"Why do we need to see the tattoo?" Minnie whispered to me.

"Could you unzip my backpack and take out the object inside?" I asked her. "And don't worry. It won't hurt you. The power is inert."

Minnie did as I asked and then sucked in a breath. "What is that doing here?"

"What is it?" Dr. Greaves asked.

"I promise you, Minnie, it won't hurt you. But we need it. It's a vital piece of evidence, and the key to getting a confession," I said.

I felt Minnie's paws shaking. She pulled out the hexed heart and dropped it on the seat before scurrying to the corner of the room.

"I can't decide if you're brave or foolish carrying that dangerous thing around." Dr. Greaves stared at the brooch, horror shifting in her gaze. "I assume you know what it is."

"I wanted to see how perfectly the engraved markings on the hexed heart fit the scar on your wrist," I said.

There was a heartbeat of silence.

"You've lost me," Dr. Greaves said slowly.

"That would be impossible," I replied. "You're a highly intelligent woman. When you fought Iona, you must have touched the brooch. It sent its energy into your flesh, leaving behind indelible evidence."

Dr. Greaves drew in a long breath. "I got this scar when I dropped an iron on my wrist. Are you happy now?"

"I'll be happy when I've fitted the hexed heart brooch onto your scar. If the markings align, then we have our killer," I said.

"This has gone too far. It's time you left. And take that wretched heart with you." Dr. Greaves stomped to the door and opened it.

Neither of us moved.

Her gaze flicked to the hexed heart, and a hungry look entered her eyes. Dr. Greaves lunged, attempting to grab it, but I swiped it up with a paw and flung it across the other side of the room.

"If you have nothing to hide, just do as I ask," I said.

"Why would the hexed heart burn you?" Minnie whispered. "Did you try to take it from Iona, and she wouldn't let it go? Did you make me lose my memory so I can't remember you being there that night?"

Dr. Greaves scowled at Minnie before turning and fleeing out the door like a bolt of shadow. I chased after her, Minnie hot on my heels.

"We have to stop her!" I hissed, but Dr. Greaves was already halfway down the corridor.

We gave chase through the morgue's halls. Cold cabinets and steel gurneys flashed past. Lights flickered above us as if reacting to the surge of magic crackling in the air.

Dr. Greaves hurled a blast of energy over her shoulder. Minnie yelped and ducked, the magic slicing the wall and leaving a scorched black scar in the plaster. Dr. Greaves turned sharply, flung open a storage door, and slammed it behind her.

I reached it a heartbeat later and launched myself at the handle, claws scrabbling. It wouldn't budge.

"She's cast a seal," Minnie panted. "I can break it, but I'll need a second."

Behind the door, glass shattered.

We backed up just as the door blew open in a shockwave of green-tinted air. The blast knocked Minnie sideways and sent me tumbling into a tray of surgical tools.

I sprang upright in time to see Dr. Greaves emerge, a potion bottle clutched in one hand, its contents glowing like swamp fire.

"Stay back," she warned, her voice trembling but eyes sharp. "Unless you want to be turned into ash like Iona, you'll do exactly what I say."

I backed up a step. "You used that to destroy Iona's body, ensuring no one would find any evidence of your involvement."

"Why did you have to poke around?" Dr. Greaves gasped.

"Because injustice is wrong," I said. "You did the preliminary investigation to make it look like you were doing your job, then added that potion to Iona's body and left it overnight. When you came back in the morning, there was nothing left of her."

Minnie hissed softly. "Iona never thought much of you. Is that why you did it? You were jealous of her abilities?"

"What did I have to be jealous of?" Dr. Greaves scoffed.

"Iona overshadowed you," Minnie said, her expression tight with fury. "You're a death doctor. She healed, but you pick over the remains."

"The remains of those she failed," Dr. Greaves sneered. "Iona wasn't perfect. She was proud and full of ego, and she thought she could save everyone. That went wrong, too."

"Iona failed to save someone you cared about?" I asked.

"The good doctor failed more than a few people," Dr. Greaves spat. "I made the mistake of recommending a friend use her services. He was never the same again."

"So, you didn't kill her out of jealousy, but because she harmed someone you cared about?" I asked.

The potion bottle wavered in Dr. Greaves's hand. "Iona always assumed she was better than she was. She needed to be brought down a peg or two."

"You didn't have to kill her to do that!" I said.

"I… I didn't mean to," Dr. Greaves said. "I asked Crispin to intensify the power in the brooch because I saw the signs of her addiction and wanted to reveal her weakness to the village. And then… then I added something else just to be sure."

"Crispin is involved," I said.

"I knew it," Minnie said.

"He asked no questions about my plan for the brooch, but, yes, he helped," Dr. Greaves said. "As I mentioned, he has a shady business and only cares about money."

"He'll care about a lot more than that once the angels are done with him," I replied.

"It's no less than he deserves," Dr. Greaves said. "But I won't be punished for a mistake."

"A mistake that killed someone," I said.

"It was such a long time ago," Dr. Greaves said. "Nobody misses Iona."

"I do!" Minnie simmered with rage.

"Can't we come to an arrangement?" Dr. Greaves's wild gaze snapped to me. "I know people who work at Angel Force. I'll put in a good word for you. Maybe get you out of here. I know that's what you want."

I tensed. "How would you manage that?"

"I have angels who owe me favors. It would be no trouble." She jerked her chin in Minnie's direction. "This familiar isn't faultless. She failed Iona. That's also a crime. Besides, you barely know her. Would you put a feeble friendship ahead of your own freedom? Your one chance of getting back home to the people you truly love?"

I wanted that. More than anything. But a glance at Minnie, who shook and glowered, confirmed I wouldn't abandon her. "You need to be punished for your crime."

"Come now, Juno. An early release from this shabby little place would make you happy. I know all about you and the witch you're bonded with. You make an extraordinary pair. Forget this nonsense in Badger's Haze. How about it?"

Minnie growled low in her throat. "Don't believe a word she says."

I didn't, even though a naïve part of me wanted to. Dr. Greaves had openly lied to me from the start of this investigation, and she'd only been helpful because she was worried I'd find out the truth about her.

A movement behind Dr. Greaves caught my eye. Baldrick and Darwin sat on the ledge, working to ease the window up with their huge shiny beaks.

"Put down the potion bottle and come with us," I said. "Angel Force already knows what's going on. Someone will be here soon to arrest you."

"I'd rather die than be arrested!" Dr. Greaves raised the potion higher, swinging her arm back, preparing to toss it at us.

Baldrick squeezed through the gap they'd made, swooped in, and grabbed the potion bottle out of her hand, causing her to scream. Darwin flew in next, circling her head and aiming pecks at her eyes.

Minnie flew into action, punching Dr. Greaves in the gut with her murder mittens, sending her to the floor.

I gave Minnie a moment to soundly thump Dr. Greaves about the head, then trotted over and rested the hexed heart on Dr. Greaves's scar.

It was a perfect fit.

# Chapter 23

"He should be here by now. Where is he?" I paced as close to the ward barrier as I dared, peering through its murky shimmer while I waited for Finn to arrive.

"He'll get there when he gets there," Sage said.

I'd brought the snow globe with me so she wouldn't miss anything. Minnie had also come along to meet Finn, although she'd been unusually quiet ever since Dr. Greaves admitted to murdering Iona. It was no surprise. She had a lot to think about.

"Maybe Cythera changed her mind," I said. "She decided not to send anyone from Angel Force."

"She has issues with you, but she'd never allow a criminal to remain unpunished," Sage said.

"Did you see Finn leave?" I asked.

"No, but I was napping after a particularly large breakfast," Sage said. "I haven't seen him around, though, so he must have left Crimson Cove by now."

"Go to Angel Force and double-check," I said.

"That would be a waste of time. Relax!"

"Impossible. Oh wait. I see something in the sky." I peered through the ward shimmer.

"There you go. I knew he'd get to you eventually," Sage said.

A warning ping of magic bounced off the barrier, making me back up as Finn landed superhero style, one fist in the dirt and his wings outstretched behind him. His feathers were a slightly darker hue than most angels, since he came with a twist of demon, but the demon mainly behaved himself.

Finn stood, brushed down his clothing, settled his wings into place, and then smiled at me.

Oh, how I'd missed that handsome, dimpled smile.

"Are you going to just stand there letting us admire you?" I bounced from paw to paw, so excited to see him.

"You need to move back. At least another ten feet," Finn said. "I get two seconds to step through the barrier before it seals again."

I wrinkled my booping snooter. "Cythera really doesn't want me to escape, does she?"

"This is her idea of a compromise," he said.

I backed away, with Minnie beside me.

"That'll do. Hold on a second." Finn placed his hand against the ward barrier, muttered a few words, and then dashed inside. It immediately shut behind him, giving me no chance to flee.

I ran at Finn and jumped onto his shoulder, weaving around his neck and curling my tail around his throat.

"It's good to see you too, buddy," Finn said, resting his hand against my side.

I introduced him to Minnie and pointed out that Sage was in the snow globe.

"So that's how you've been communicating," Finn said. "You'd better keep that quiet or Cythera will insist I take it away."

"I refuse to be entirely cut off from Crimson Cove," I said. "Badger's Haze is not a friendly place."

"And she missed talking to me," Sage said.

"Maybe that too," I replied.

"I don't have long, so you'd better show me where you've got Dr. Greaves stashed," Finn said.

"We trapped her in her office," I said. "Minnie helped with a containment spell. We also knocked her out with magic to make sure she did nothing nefarious."

"You cast that spell?" Finn asked.

"No, my magic is still back in Crimson Cove, but I'm learning a few tricks so I can get by," I said.

Finn chuckled. "I figured you would. Nothing can keep you down for long."

I pointed out where the office was, and we hurried that way. A device on Finn's wrist buzzed, and he sighed as he checked it.

"What's that?" I asked.

"Cythera is keeping tabs on me," he said. "I can stay for ten minutes before magic drags me out. She told me to get in, collect the criminal, and leave. I'm not supposed to talk to you."

"She really hates me." I hissed softly. "Even after I've solved these cold cases for her. She knows how to hold a grudge."

"I'm not arguing with that," Finn said. "You didn't make her look too good, though. Angels aren't supposed to be prideful, but she has a healthy dose."

"She's not even debating with the higher angels about the mistake they made in banishing me here?" I asked.

"Cythera is obeying their orders. It's what she always does," Finn said.

"Even though they're wrong," I muttered.

We reached the office, and Finn pulled open the door. Minnie followed, dragging the snow globe behind on a small trolley we'd taken from the library.

As soon as the door shut, Finn reached up and slipped a small piece of paper under one paw. "Read that later, and in secret. It could help your situation."

I gripped the paper tight with my claws, a tickle of excited anticipation inside me. Was it a way out of Badger's Haze?

We reached Dr. Greaves's office to find her stirring from the knockout spell we'd covered her with.

She looked at us with groggy eyes. "What's going on?"

"You're about to go away for a very long time for murder," I said.

Finn introduced himself. "You're to come with me. We'll question you, take your confession, and then process the evidence."

"You can't trust the word of that foul feline," Dr. Greaves said spitefully. "You sent her here because she's unhinged. And there's something strange about the magic that lingers on her."

"This isn't about Juno's punishment. We've been informed of the evidence collected against you," Finn said.

"How is that possible?" Dr. Greaves struggled to her feet and smoothed her hands over her crumpled clothing. "I thought that cat was banished here because she messed with Angel Force. Her powers were taken."

"We have our ways." Finn winked at me discreetly. "And the evidence on your wrist is damning. If the hexed heart touched you when you had dark intent, we'll find a residual record in its magic. Nobody will deny that evidence."

She huffed out a breath. "I knew I should have destroyed that thing."

"You're admitting what you did?" Finn asked.

"Dr. Greaves has already made her confession to us, and I have a recording spell on me, so there's a record of our conversation," I said. "She added something to the brooch that made it unstable. That's what killed Iona."

Dr. Greaves's shoulders slumped. "I'm a valuable member of this magic forsaken community. I haven't put a foot wrong since that unfortunate accident. Surely that counts for something."

"I doubt Iona would see it that way," Minnie said. "You deserve everything that's coming to you."

Finn restrained Dr. Greaves with a golden loop of angel tether, ensuring she wouldn't escape while he transported her to Crimson Cove to answer for her crime.

I waited on the desk, still clutching the piece of paper, eager to see what was written on it.

The device on Finn's wrist buzzed again. "Time's up. I need to get out of here. Thanks, Juno. We appreciate your help in solving these cases."

"Does that include Cythera?" I asked as I followed him along the corridor, Dr. Greaves in tow. "Does what I'm doing mean anything to her?"

"It means something to the victims who never got justice," Finn said.

"Yes. And that's definitely important," I replied. "But does Cythera know I'm making amends? Not that I'm saying I have anything to make amends for. It was those higher angels who made a mistake, but I can make Crimson Cove a better place. A safer place. Isn't that what Cythera wants?"

"Sure, it is." Finn pushed open the door and led Dr. Greaves outside. "Just give it more time. I'll make sure she doesn't forget you."

"She'd like to," I said.

"Yes. Perhaps so. But solving these cold cases is worthwhile. Besides, what else would you do? Take naps and eat lots of snacks?" Finn asked.

"The library ghosts make sure napping isn't easy," I said. "And the snacks in this town are sorely lacking."

"Oh! I almost forgot." Finn reached inside his feathers and pulled out a packet of smoked salmon. "A gift from Sorcha. Enjoy."

My mouth watered as I admired the succulent strips of salmon.

Minnie nosed at the package. "Yum. That looks even better than tinned ham."

I batted her away with a paw. "I've been dreaming of this salmon."

"No one's forgetting you in Crimson Cove," Finn said. "We're all working to get you back. The wheels of justice turn slowly."

"They wouldn't turn slowly if I were there." I resisted the urge to rip into the packet of salmon and gobble it down.

"You'll be back home soon," Finn said.

"How soon?" I asked.

He shrugged. "I wish I could be more helpful."

"At least tell me about Zandra," I said. "How's she doing?"

Finn opened his mouth and then snapped it shut. He groaned and tipped his head back to stare at the sky.

"What's wrong?" I asked. "Is something the matter with Zandra?"

He drew in a breath. "It's not that. It's just that I can't talk about—" His mouth clamped shut again.

I hissed my frustration. "Has Cythera put a spell on you so you can't tell me anything about my witch?"

Finn nodded, an apologetic look in his eyes. "Sorry, but it's part of your punishment. Cythera even refused to let Zandra send you anything. That's why I snuck in the salmon. It's really from Zandra, but Sorcha had to give it to me so we could get around the rules."

"I never knew angels could be so cruel," I said.

"You know what the higher angels can be like. They have a weird logic. They tell Cythera to do something, or not let you see or have things, and she agrees," Finn replied. "I've really got to go. The last thing I want is to be yanked out of here by Cythera's magic and reprimanded. She'd put me on night duty for the next month as punishment."

"Cythera sounds under stress," I said. "If only she had the sense to let me back home, I'd take all of that off her shoulders."

"I agree. Things haven't been the same in Crimson Cove since you left," Finn said.

"I heard a rumor there's trouble with the magic," I said. "Is there anything I can help with?"

"I'm sure you could, if you were there," Finn said. "Something's going on, but we can't figure out what it is."

My heart flipped over. "What kind of thing?"

Finn's wrist device buzzed angrily. "I'm on my last few seconds. Take care, Juno. And I hope to see you soon." He ran at the barrier, one arm clamping Dr. Greaves against his chest, and the other held up so he could break through with magic before it reformed behind him.

I stood with Minnie, and we watched him leave. Frustration swirled inside me. What was going on back home? Finn had been about to tell me something important, but Cythera's foolish rules and inability to see beyond the higher angels' orders had ruined things.

"I forgot how handsome those angels were," Minnie said. "He's dreamy."

"Finn's the best," I said. "Unfortunately, he's got a boss for a tyrant, and she's got higher angels who are just as cruel. I wish I knew what was going on back home."

"At least you have a home." There was a forlorn note in Minnie's voice.

I turned to look at her. "You don't see Badger's Haze as your home anymore?"

"What's the point of being here?" Minnie asked. "I stuck around because I had unfinished business. That business has been solved."

"Which is good. We resolved a long-standing mystery that stopped you from finding peace."

"Yeah, you did. And thanks. I'm glad I know what happened," Minnie said. "I wish it hadn't, but at least the truth is out and Dr. Greaves will be punished."

"If you're not staying here, what will you do now?" I asked. "Do you have family or friends you could stay with?"

"I... I was thinking of going to Morticia and seeing if there was space for me," Minnie said.

"By space, you mean a grave?" I shook my head. "You've survived all these years without having a bond with a magic user. That shows how strong you are."

"I got my resolution," Minnie said. "And that's it. I've achieved my last dream. Besides, I only survived because I was taking magic that didn't belong to me. That's wrong, and no way to live."

"Don't give up. You could bond with someone else. Or you could stay on your own and work on your abilities. Then, should a magic user come along who's a good fit for you, you'd be ready for them."

"That sounds like a lot of work," Minnie said. "And there's no guarantee I'll meet anyone who comes close to Iona."

"Give it some more thought," I replied. "While you do, I've got that packet of succulent salmon that needs eating." My gaze shifted to the glorious packet of fishy heaven resting in the trolley next to the snow globe.

"There's no way you're sharing that with me. You whacked me around the face when I tried to take a sniff," Minnie said.

"I'm protective of my salmon," I replied. "Come back to the library. We can share it and see if there's a space that might suit you while you figure things out."

"You're asking me to move in with you for good?" Minnie asked.

"Why not? It can be as short-term or as long-term as you like," I said. "And there's plenty of room, so we won't bump into each other if you need your space to figure things out. And I'm always around if you want to talk things through."

"That's not a terrible idea," Minnie said.

"And there are plenty of research materials in the library," Sage said from the snow globe. "Maybe you'll find an interest to keep you going. And Juno needs all the help she can get with her terrible magic practice. She's so lazy."

"I'm not lazy! I'm just used to doing things differently. It takes time to adjust."

"I enjoy mixing ingredients and making potions," Minnie said. "I did it with Iona. We'd spend hours brewing the perfect tinctures and lotions for her clients to use. It was so satisfying."

"There you go. You're the perfect fit," Sage said. "Minnie, you move into the library, sort Juno out, and while you're at it, you can figure out what you want to do with the rest of your life."

"Hmmm, that's hardly a small thing to puzzle through," Minnie said.

"One paw step forward at a time," I said. "And it's the journey, not the destination, you need to focus on. That's where true happiness lies. What do you say, Minnie? We'll take it one day at a time. Starting with this salmon."

"Okay. I'll give it a go," Minnie said.

We headed back to the library, Minnie still towing Sage behind her. We'd just settled in and were about to explore to find the perfect room for Minnie when there was a knock at the main door.

I hurried over and unbolted it to discover three of the suspects in the investigation standing outside.

Delphine held a cake. Hester had a box of bottles of alcohol, and Lavender carried a tray of brownies with green frosting.

"What's this?" I asked.

"We wanted to thank you for figuring out what happened to Iona." Lavender wiggled the tray of brownies. "You've got to try these. I made them myself. You'll be bouncing off the walls for days."

"This box is heavy," Hester said. "Are you inviting us in or not?"

"Of course. You're welcome." I stood back, shocked by the unexpected kindness. After all, I'd viewed everyone coming through the door as a potential murderer.

"We were going to invite Crispin to join us." Delphine ambled past me, sucking chocolate frosting off her finger, "but when Lavender stopped by, his store was empty."

"He's fled Badger's Haze?" I asked.

"I guess. His nasty little schemes must have finally caught up with him."

"Angel Force will be after him," I said. "He helped Dr. Greaves with her plan to destabilize the magic in the hexed heart."

"Good. I hope they catch that sneaky jerk and put him away," Hester said as she thumped down her box. "He always made my skin crawl."

I hopped onto the table beside her. "I imagine the people you blackmail feel the same way about you."

She slid me a glare from the corner of her eye. "You lost me."

"I have your little book of blackmailing secrets."

Hester turned to me, her hands clenched. "How in the hell—"

"No, not another word from you. Listen to me," I said. "If you don't start treating your amazing ravens with respect and kindness, that spite-filled journal will find its way to Angel Force. They don't look kindly on blackmailers."

"Don't blab to the angels." Hester loomed over me. "And I do what I have to. Those birds need controlling."

"Use the carrot not the stick method from now on. Kindness first, or your freedom will be taken away. Do we have a deal?"

"If I agree, do I get my journal back?"

"No. The blackmail ends. The villagers have enough problems without glancing over their shoulders to ensure you aren't snooping on them."

"If they did nothing wrong, they wouldn't have to worry," Hester said.

"Be better, Hester. Set an example. Use your ravens to find lost things, watch the wards to ensure they stay stable, and give them time off. Offer them kindness and they'll return it," I said.

I got another glare and then a curt nod. Hester needed watching, but I was hopeful she'd turn over a new leaf.

After hopping off the desk, I was about to shut the door when Roland appeared. He looked healthy. His fur gleamed, his eyes were bright, and his tail was up.

"Is this your doing?" I asked him.

He shook his head. "No, but I got an invitation, so thought I'd stop by. I'm sorry I haven't been by after everything that happened, but it's been busy."

"I'm glad to see you," I said. "Come in and celebrate. We just solved another cold case."

"I heard. Thanks, but I can't stay for long," Roland said. "I'm living with Tabitha now, and we're sorting out a home of our own. We decided we didn't want to live with the ghosts of our past, so we're investigating new spaces. We've found nothing suitable yet, but there are plenty of abandoned buildings to explore."

"If you're interested, I've got a library," I said. "Well, Minnie is moving in, but you and Tabitha are welcome here, too. The top floor may suit you."

He glanced up. "Huh. There's an idea. Thanks. I'll bring her by in a day or two, and we'll look around."

"Stop talking and let's party!" Lavender called out, a half-eaten brownie already in one hand and a bottle of beer in the other.

"I'd better go. Enjoy your party," Roland said. "You've earned it."

Within ten minutes, a party atmosphere filled the library, sweeping away the musty silence. The ghosts even got involved, swirling around, telling jokes, and dancing to the music Sage played through the snow globe.

It was an astonishing sight and made me feel there was still a possibility that Badger's Haze could rise again and be redeemed. Maybe my time here would help to achieve that in some small part.

Before joining the party, I snuck to a quiet spot and opened the slip of paper Finn had given me. I recognized his messy handwriting immediately.

*Cythera's great-great-aunt died mysteriously in Badger's Haze. Find out why.*

I sucked in a breath, and my heart pitter-pattered. I'd just gotten my ticket home.

# About the author

K.E. O'Connor (Karen) is a cozy mystery author living in the beautiful British countryside. She loves all things mystery, animals, and cake.

When she's not writing, she volunteers at a local animal sanctuary, reads a ton of books, binge watches mystery series, and dreams of living somewhere warmer.

To stay in touch with the mysteries, where the killer always gets caught, justice is served magic style, and the familiars talk, join her newsletter.

**Newsletter:**
www.subscribepage.com/cozymysteries
**Website:** www.keoconnor.com
**Facebook:** www.facebook.com/keoconnorauthor

www.ingramcontent.com/pod-product-compliance
Lightning Source LLC
Chambersburg PA
CBHW050611190726
48283CB00007B/2374